THE ROVE
IN SOUTHERN

CW01082634

OR

THE DESERTED STEAM YACHT

BY
ARTHUR M. WINFIELD

NEW WEST PRESS

New West Press
Henderson, NV 89052
www.nwwst com

Ordering Information:
Special discounts are available on quantity purchases by corporations, associations, educators, and others. For details, contact the publisher at the listed address below.

U.S. trade bookstores and wholesalers: Please contact New West Press:

Tel: (480) 648-1061; or email: contact@nwwst.com

INTRODUCTION

My Dear Boys: "The Rover Boys in Southern Waters" is a complete story in itself but forms the eleventh volume of a line known by the general title of "The Rover Boys Series for Young Americans."

Eleven volumes! Just think of it! What a great number to write about one set of young people and their doings! When I started out, as I have mentioned before, I thought to pen three volumes, possibly four. I was not at all sure that the boys and girls would wish any of them. But no sooner had I given them "The Rover Boys at School" than there was a demand for "The Rover Boys on the Ocean" and then "The Rover Boys in the Jungle," and then, year after year, there followed "The Rover Boys Out West," "On the Great Lakes," "In the Mountains," "On Land and Sea," "In Camp," "On the River," and "On the Plains," where we last met them.

In the present tale the scene is shifted to the lower Mississippi and then the Gulf of Mexico. As before, Sam, Tom, and Dick are introduced, along with a number of their friends, and all have a variety of adventures and not a little fun. While on the Gulf the boys discover a deserted steam yacht, board the craft, and try to ascertain who is the owner, and this leads to a mystery which I leave the pages that follow to unfold.

Once again I take the opportunity to thank the thousands of young folks all over our broad land who have signified their appreciation of my efforts to afford them amusement and at the same time teach a moral. Were it possible I should like nothing better than to write to each and shake everyone by the hand. But that is out of the question, so I can simply pen my thanks, and subscribe myself,

Affectionately and sincerely yours,

EDWARD STRATEMEYER

CONTENTS

ON THE TOP OF THIS AFFAIR STOOD A CAMPSTOOL, AND ON
THE STOOL SAT OM ROVER.

CHAPTER I

THE ROVER BOYS AND THEIR FRIENDS

"The houseboat is gone!"

"Tom, what do you mean?"

"I mean just what I say, Sam. The houseboat is gone—vanished, missing, disappeared, drifted away, stolen!" ejaculated Tom Rover, excitedly.

"Tom, don't go on in such a crazy fashion. Do you mean to say the houseboat isn't where we left it?"

"It is not,—and it is nowhere in sight on the river," returned Tom Rover. "Come, we must tell Dick and the others about this."

"But we left the Dora in charge of that big planter last night," insisted the youngest of the Rover boys. "He said he would take good care of the craft."

"Well, he is gone too. I hunted high and low for the houseboat, and for that planter, but without success."

"Maybe the boat drifted away, with the planter on board, Tom. The current has been pretty strong since those heavy rains."

"She was tied up good and tight," answered Tom Rover, his usually merry face wearing a troubled look. "I can't understand it."

"I must say I didn't like that planter's manner much. He looked to be rather a sly one. Come on, let us find Dick and the others at once," went on Sam Rover. "If the houseboat has been stolen we want to know it right away, so we can get on the trail of the thief."

"True for you, Sam." Tom Rover heaved a short sigh. "My! what a lot of troubles we have had since we started on this houseboat trip!"

"Yes—but we have had lots of sport too."

The two brothers were standing near the bank of the broad Mississippi River, just below the town of Shapette, in Louisiana. The party to which they belonged had reached the town on their journey down the Father of Waters the day before, and an hour later the houseboat had been tied up at a bend in the stream and left in charge of a planter who had appeared and volunteered for the task. The planter had given his name as Gasper Pold, and had stated that his plantation lay half a mile inland, on higher ground. He had mentioned several people in Shapette as being his close friends—among others the principal storekeeper—and the boys had thought it all right to get him to look after the houseboat while they paid a visit to a sugar plantation where one of their party had a distant relative living.

To my old readers the Rover boys, Sam, Tom, and Dick, need no special introduction. Sam was the youngest, fun-loving Tom next, and cool-headed and clever Dick the oldest.

When at home the three boys lived with their father, Anderson Rover, and their uncle Randolph and aunt Martha in a pleasant portion of New York State called Valley Brook, near the village of Dexter's Corners. From that home they had gone, as already related in "The Rover Boys at School," to Putnam Hall, an ideal place of learning, where they made many friends and also some enemies.

A term at school had been followed by a brief trip on the Atlantic Ocean, and then a journey to the jungles of Africa, where the lads went in a hunt for their father, who had become lost. Then they had gone west, to establish a family claim to a valuable mine, and afterwards taken two well-deserved outings, one on the Great Lakes and the other in the mountains.

From the mountains the Rover boys had expected to go back to Putnam Hall, but a scarlet fever scare caused a temporary closing of that institution of learning and the lads took a trip to the Pacific coast and were cast away on the ocean, as told of in "The Rover Boys on Land and Sea," the seventh volume of this series. But all came back safely and returned to the Hall, there to do their duty and have considerable fun, as set forth in "The Rover Boys in Camp."

The boys' uncle, Randolph Rover, had taken an elegant houseboat for debt. This craft was located on the Ohio River, and in a volume called "The Rover Boys on the River," I related how Sam, Tom, and Dick resolved to take a trip on the craft during their summer vacation. On this outing they were accompanied by "Songbird" Powell, a school chum given to the making of doggerel which he persisted in calling poetry, Fred Garrison, who had stood by the Rovers through thick and thin, and Hans Mueller, a German youth who had not yet fully mastered the English language. To make the trip more interesting the boys invited an old friend, Mrs. Stanhope, to accompany them, and also Mrs. Laning, her sister. With Mrs. Stanhope was a daughter Dora, who Dick Rover thought was the best and sweetest girl in the whole world, and with Mrs. Laning were her daughters Grace and Nellie, warm friends of Tom and Sam.

The trip on the houseboat started well enough, but soon came trouble through the underhanded work of Dan Baxter, a big youth who had been the Rovers' bitter enemy ever since they had gone to Putnam Hall, and another boy named Lew Flapp. These young rascals ran off with the houseboat and two of the girls, and it took hard work to regain the craft and come to the girls' rescue. Lew Flapp was made a prisoner and sent east to stand trial for some of his numerous misdeeds, but Dan Baxter escaped.

"We don't want to see any more of Baxter," Sam had said, but this wish was not to be gratified. Floating down the Mississippi, the houseboat got damaged in a big storm, and had to be laid up for repairs. This being so, all on board decided to take a trip inland, and accordingly they set out, the ladies and girls by way of the railroad and the boys on horseback.

As already told in "The Rover Boys on the Plains," this trip was full of mystery and peril. Dan Baxter turned up most unexpectedly, and our friends visited a mysterious ranch only to learn that it was a rendezvous for a band of counterfeiters. Through a government detective the counterfeiters were rounded up, only one man, Sack Todd, escaping. Dan Baxter also got away, but later on he was traced to a big swamp, where his horse was found, stuck fast in the slimy ooze. It was thought by some that Baxter had lost his life trying to find his way through the swamp, but of this the Rovers were somewhat doubtful.

After the capture of the counterfeiters the boys and their chums had gone on to meet the ladies and the girls, and had spent a full week at the ranch of a friend, having the best times possible, horseback riding, hunting, and helping to round-up cattle. Then the whole party had gone back to the Mississippi, embarked on the Dora, as the houseboat was named, and floated down the mighty stream once more.

"This sort of thing is simply grand," Fred Garrison had remarked, as he stood on the forward deck of the craft, yet an hour later he had changed his tune. The houseboat had gone whirling in a bend of the stream, struck a snag and hurled poor Fred overboard. He was hauled up by Sam and Dick Rover, and then it was ascertained that the houseboat was leaking and would have to be laid up again for repairs.

They had stopped at the town of Shapette, a small place, and there they found a carpenter who promised to do what they wanted. When the houseboat was laid up the captain had come to them with a letter.

"My brother in Cairo is dead," said Captain Starr. "I shall have to leave you and look after his children."

The captain was an eccentric individual and the Rovers did not like him much, so they were perfectly willing to let him go. They decided to look around for somebody else to manage the houseboat and in the meantime run the craft themselves.

With the party as cook and general housekeeper was Alexander Pop, a colored man who had once been a waiter at Putnam Hall, but who was now attached to the Rover household. The boys had expected to leave Aleck, as he was called, in charge of the Dora while they visited a nearby sugar plantation, but the colored man had begged to be taken along, "jes fo' de change," as he expressed it. As Aleck had remained on the houseboat during the entire time the boys were on the plains Dick agreed to take him along; and thus, for the time being, the Dora had been left in the sole care of the planter.

After the visit to the sugar plantation the party had ridden to Shapette, to do a little shopping before returning to the houseboat. There Tom and Sam had left the others, to make certain that the Dora was in proper trim to continue the trip down the Mississippi. On the way Sam stopped at a plantation house to get a drink of water, and when he rejoined his brother it was to learn the dismaying news that the houseboat and the man left in charge of the craft had mysteriously disappeared.

CHAPTER II

ABOUT A MISSING HOUSEBOAT

"Let us go down the river and see if the Dora is behind yonder trees," suggested Sam, after he had had time to digest what his brother had said.

"All right, if you say so," answered Tom. "But I feel it in my bones it won't do any good."

The two brothers ran along the wet and slippery bank of the river, which at this point sprawled out into almost a lake. They had to walk around several wet places and were pretty well out of wind by the time they gained the patch of wood the youngest Rover had pointed out. They ran to a point where they could get a clear view of the stream for a full mile.

"Gone—just as I told you," said Tom, laconically.

"Oh, Tom, do you really think that planter stole the houseboat?"

"I don't know what to think, to tell the truth. We have fallen in with all kinds of evil characters since we began this trip."

"Even if we go back to Dick and the others and tell them, what good will it do?"

"I don't really know. But I am going to tell Dick, just as fast as I can."

There seemed really nothing else to do, and with heavy hearts Sam and Tom retraced their steps to where the Dora had been tied up, and started to return to town.

"This will certainly worry the ladies and the girls a good deal," observed Sam, as they hurried along. "If the houseboat is gone, we can't continue the trip."

"They won't be worried any more than we are, Sam. It's hard lines all around. If that planter really stole the boat he ought to suffer for it."

"Just what I say."

The brothers soon came in sight of Shapette,—a small settlement where half of the inhabitants were of French extraction. As they reached one of the streets they heard a cheerful whistle.

"That's Dick!" said Sam. "He won't whistle so happily when he learns the news."

"Hullo!" came from Dick Rover, as he caught sight of his brothers. "What brings you back so soon?"

"Thought you were going to stay on the houseboat until we got there," added Fred Garrison, who, with Hans Mueller, accompanied the eldest Rover.

"There is no houseboat to stay on," answered Tom.

"What!"

"The houseboat is gone—and so is that planter who said he'd take care of her."

"Mine cracious me!" burst out Hans Mueller. "You ton't tole me alretty!"

"Tom, you don't mean—" Dick paused.

"The houseboat is gone, clean and clear, Dick."

"And that planter, Gasper Pold—"

"Is gone too," returned Sam. "And so is that carpenter who said he'd repair the craft."

"This is certainly too bad. Tell me the particulars," and Dick's face grew decidedly serious.

"There isn't much to tell," said Tom. "We got there, looked around, made a search, and here we are. No boat in sight, no person to be seen, just nothing and nobody."

"But the houseboat must be somewhere, Tom."

"I agree with you, but not being a second-sight mind reader I can't tell you where."

Alexander Pop, who was with the boys, had listened closely with his eyes rolling in wonder.

"Fo' de lan' sakes!" he ejaculated. "Dat's de wuss news I's heard in a long time. Seems lak da was no end of troubles fo' dis crowd!"

"Well, if this doesn't beat the Dutch!" murmured Fred Garrison.

"Yah, und it beats der Irish too alretty!" came from Hans Mueller. "Chust ven ve dink der sthars vos shinin' it begins to rain; eh, ain't dot so?"

"You've struck the nail on the head, Hans," answered Sam. "I thought we'd have plain sailing from to-day, and now it looks as if we'd have no sailing at all!"

"Boys," spoke up Dick, sharply, "if that houseboat has been stolen we must get the craft back."

"So say I, Dick," answered Tom. "But how are you going to begin about it?"

"That remains to be seen. Of one thing I am pretty certain—if the houseboat went anywhere it went down the stream. Only a powerful tug or steamboat could pull such a boat up this mighty river."

"That's true—and we must look down the Mississippi for the craft," said Fred.

"Where is Songbird?" asked Tom.

"I left him with the ladies and the girls. They will be along presently, in a carriage," answered Dick.

"There won't be any use of the ladies and girls going down to the river, so long as the Dora is missing," said Sam. "They'll have to stay in town, or go back to that sugar plantation, until we learn about the craft."

It was decided that Sam should join the other crowd and acquaint them with the news. He found them at one of the stores, where Mrs. Stanhope was buying some embroidery silk.

"Have you got tired of waiting for us, Sam?" asked Grace Laning, who was the first to see the youngest Rover.

"Oh, I've got bad news, Grace." And then he told the girl of what had occurred, in the midst of which the others came up.

"Missing again!" ejaculated Songbird Powell. "Too bad! What's to be done?"

"We don't know yet."

The ladies were much alarmed and so were the girls. Sam did what he could to quiet their fears, yet he felt unhappy himself.

"I did not like the looks of that planter at all," declared Dora Stanhope. "He had the face of a sneak. I was going to speak to Dick about it, and I am sorry now that I didn't."

"I presume we shall have to remain here until you find the houseboat," came from Mrs. Laning.

"Either here or at the sugar plantation," answered Sam.

"What will you do?"

"I don't know yet—probably go down the river and look for the Dora. She is so large they can't hide her very well."

"Maybe the current of the river carried her away and the planter got scared and left," suggested Songbird. "You'll remember, she broke away once before."

"She couldn't break away—she was tied up good and tight," answered Sam, decidedly.

"Well, if you cannot find the houseboat, we'll have to go home from here instead of from New Orleans," said Mrs. Stanhope. "That will shorten our trip somewhat but not a great deal. But I hope, for your uncle's sake, that you get his property back."

"We'll do that, or know the reason why," answered Sam.

"What's this trouble about your houseboat?" asked the storekeeper, who had caught part of the conversation.

"It's missing."

"So you said. Too bad!"

"Do you know the planter who had charge of the craft?" went on Sam. "He was tall and thin and went by the name of Gasper Pold."

"What, did you leave your boat with that man? You should have known better. Didn't you know Pold was an old lottery sharp?"

"We did not."

"Well, he is, and has cheated many a poor white man and nigger out of his hard-earned savings. He's in bad flavor around here, and some of the citizens were just about to ask him to leave or run the risk of tar and feathers."

"Well, he has left, and taken our houseboat with him," said Sam, bitterly. "What about Solly Jackson, the carpenter who was going to do some repairs for us?"

"Oh, Solly's a fairly good kind, but years ago he used to work the lottery ticket game with Pold. He's an old bachelor and never has much to say about anything."

"Has he any regular shop?"

"Oh, no; he's a come-day-go-day sort of fellow, boards around, and like that."

"Then he must be in with Gasper Pold," said the youngest Rover. "They've cleared out together with our property."

"Hum! Might be so, lad. Have much on board the craft?"

"Yes, a great many things—furniture, a piano, books, and all of our clothing."

"Hum! Quite a haul—if they can get away with it. Maybe you had better notify the authorities."

"We certainly will—if we can't find the houseboat," said Sam, and then, after a few words more with the ladies and the girls, he started off to rejoin Tom and Dick, and Songbird Powell went with him.

CHAPTER III

A FRIEND IN NEED

It was ten o'clock in the morning when the discovery was made that the houseboat was missing, and by the middle of the afternoon the Rover boys and their chums were certain that the craft had been stolen by Gasper Pold and Solly Jackson.

A negro boy who went by the name of Wash—evidently short for Washington—gave them more information than anybody else. This boy, who had been fishing near the woods below Shapette, stated that he had seen the two men go aboard the houseboat early in the morning, accompanied by a young man who was a stranger. The three had cast off the ropes, poled the houseboat far out into the stream, and then drifted out of sight down the mighty Mississippi.

"I thought dat it was werry funny da should be gwine away," said the young darkey. "But I didn't dare to go show myself, fo' I know dat Gasper Pold is a bad aig when he's riled up, yes, sah!"

"You didn't know the young man who went along?" asked Dick.

"No, sah—neber see him afoah, sah."

"How did he look?"

"He looked putty much lak a tramp, yes, sah! He was putty dirty too, he was!"

"Some tramp they got to help them," was Tom's comment. "The question is, Where will they go with the houseboat?"

"I don't think they'll dare to go to any of the big towns," said Dick. "They'll be afraid we'll telegraph ahead to catch them. More than likely they'll land at some out-of-the-way spot and cart our valuables off in a wagon. Then possibly they'll cast the houseboat adrift, or set fire to her."

"If that's the case, what's to do?" questioned Fred Garrison. "I hate to sit still and do nothing."

"Yah! let us go after dem fellers mit pitchforks alretty!" added Hans, vehemently. "Such robbers ought to peen electrocutioned mit a rope, ain't dot so?"

"You mean hung, Hans," said Sam. "They certainly ought to be punished.

> "Well swing them high, I do declare,
> And let them dance on naught but air!
> And When they've danced and hour so slick,
> We'll cut them down and bury them quick,"

came softly from Songbird, who could not resist the temptation to burst into verse.

"Great shoestrings, Songbird! To think you'd make up poetry on such a subject," cried Fred.

"Couldn't help it—I haven't composed anything to-day," was the calm answer.

"Maype Songpird been komposing boultry ven he been in his coffin," remarked Hans.

"All of which doesn't answer the question, What are we going to do?" said Sam.

"I wonder if I can charter a small tug or steamboat to go down the river after the houseboat," came from Dick.

"There isn't much to be had in the town," answered Fred Garrison. "Still, we can try."

The Rovers with their friends returned to Shapette. Here they ran into the chief of police, who also acted as a sort of detective.

"Boat stolen! Is it possible!" burst out that official. "Never heard of such a thing befo', sah, never! I am sorry, sah, exceedingly sorry, sah! Have you any idea who is guilty, sah?"

"I have," answered Dick, and told what he knew.

"A bad man, sah, that Gasper Pold—ought to have been arrested long ago, sah, yes, sah. But nobody would make a complaint—all afraid of a shooting—very quick man to draw a pistol, yes, sah."

"That's interesting," said Tom. "He'll be a fine man to confront, if we catch up to him."

The chief of police said he would do anything he could, but in the end refused to leave Shapette, and so did nothing. The Rovers soon learned that all he was good for was to talk, and they left him in disgust.

"We must take this trail up ourselves," said Sam. "And the quicker the better."

They walked down to the river front, and after a number of inquiries found out that to charter a tug or small steamboat was just then out of the question, for no craft of that sort was near. But they learned that a young man of the vicinity named Harold Bird, who was the owner of several valuable plantations in that district, owned a new gasoline launch of good size which was housed at a place a mile away.

"I am going to see Harold Bird," said Dick. "Perhaps he'll lend us his launch."

They found out where the young man lived and visited the plantation in a carriage. It was a beautiful place, with an old family mansion surrounded by grounds laid out with exquisite taste.

"Evidently these folks have money," observed Tom.

"Oh, some of these planters are immensely wealthy," answered Sam.

As they drove into the grounds they saw a young man playing with a bird dog on the lawn. He smiled at them pleasantly.

"Is this Mr. Harold Bird?" asked Dick.

"Yes," was the reply. "What can I do for you?"

"Let me introduce myself, Mr. Bird. I am Dick Rover, and these are my brothers. Sam and Tom. These are my friends, Fred Garrison and John Powell."

"Is it possible!" exclaimed Harold Bird. "Why, I was reading about you only yesterday, in the newspaper. You are the young fellows who helped to round up that gang of counterfeiters at Red Rock ranch.

It was certainly a stirring piece of work. You deserve a great deal of credit." And then the young Southerner shook hands all around.

"Mr. Bird, we are in trouble," went on Dick, "and we thought that perhaps you would be able to help us out."

"I will certainly do anything that I possibly can for you. Come, sit down and tell me what is wrong."

The young Southerner led the way to the broad veranda, and all took seats. Then Dick and the others told about the missing house-boat and of how they had wanted to charter a tug or a steamboat to go in pursuit.

"I could not find a vessel of any kind," said Dick. "But some folks told me that you had a big gasoline launch, and I thought perhaps you would let us have that. Of course we'll pay you for—"

"Never mind about pay, Mr. Rover. I shall be glad to be of service to you. I will let you have my launch on one condition."

"And that is—"

"That you will take me with you. I love excitement, and this pursuit of those rascals is just to my taste. We can take one of my best dogs along, so, if we find they have landed anywhere, we can readily trace them."

"But the danger?" said Sam.

"Why should I be afraid if you are not? Of course you will go well armed."

"Indeed we will," said Tom. "More than likely they'll be well armed, too."

After that a long talk ensued, and Harold Bird had the servants treat the boys to light refreshments. He was a capital fellow, with a winning, though rather sad smile, and all liked him from the start.

"I've seen a bit of adventure myself,—visiting Mexico and Europe, and climbing high mountains," he said. "But I haven't had such stirring times as you. It is very quiet here, and I shall enjoy the change."

"Are you alone here, may I ask?" said Fred, curiously.

"Yes, excepting for my overseer and the servants. The estate was left to me by my mother, who died three years ago."

"It must be rather lonely," murmured Songbird.

"It is exceedingly lonely at times, and that is why I travel a great deal—that and for another reason." And the face of the young man clouded for the time. Evidently he had something on his mind, but what it was he did not just then mention.

He told them how he had come to buy the gasoline launch and said it was big enough to take on board a party of twelve or fifteen with comfort. It was decided to take some provisions along, for there was no telling how long the chase would last.

It was evening before all arrangements were completed and the whole party went to town. There they met the ladies and the girls, and Harold Bird was introduced.

"I should consider it an honor to have you remain at my plantation while we are off on this search for the houseboat," said the young Southerner. "You can stay there as long as you please and make yourselves thoroughly at home."

As there was no good hotel in the town, this invitation relieved Mrs. Stanhope and Mrs. Laning a great deal, and they said they would accept the offer, and thanked the young man very much. Carriages were obtained, and inside of two hours the ladies and the girls were at Lee Hall, as Harold Bird called his place. There were rooms in plenty for all, and each was made to feel perfectly at home. It was decided that Aleck Pop should also remain at the plantation for the time being.

"The hospitality in the South is certainly marvelous," said Dora to Dick. "When I left home I never thought I should be treated so well."

"You are right, Dora. The whole world over, you will find no greater gentleman than one from our South."

"And what a beautiful plantation!" cried Nellie. "What grand walks, and trees and flowers!"

"And what a fine lot of colored servants," came from Grace. "Really they won't let me do a thing for myself!"

"I should think Mr. Bird would be very happy," said Mrs. Laning, for at that moment the owner of the estate was not present.

"You'd think so," answered Dick. "But do you know, notwith-standing his smiling face he appears at times to be very sad."

"I thought so," said Mrs. Stanhope. "He acts as if he had some-thing on his mind."

"Yes, and something that worried him a great deal," added Tom.

They were right, Harold Bird had a great deal to worry him, and what it was we shall learn as our tale proceeds.

CHAPTER IV

HAROLD BIRD'S STRANGE TALE

Early in the morning the Rovers and their friends were ready to take their departure. Dick came down in the garden at sunrise, and was soon joined by Dora, and they took a short walk together.

"Oh, Dick, you must keep out of danger," said Dora. "Promise me you will be careful!"

"I will be careful, Dora," he answered, as he looked down into the depths of her clear eyes. "I will be careful—for your sake," he added, in almost a whisper.

"If something sh—should happen to you!" she faltered.

"I'll take care of myself, don't fear, Dora," he made reply, and then, as they were all alone he drew her up to him. "Dora, may I?" he asked, softly and tenderly.

She did not answer, but looked up at him, innocently and confidingly. He bent over and kissed her, and gave her hand a little squeeze.

"We understand each other, don't we, Dora?" he whispered.

"Of course we do," she whispered in return.

"And some day you'll be Mrs. Dick Rover?"

"Oh, Dick!"

"But you will be, won't you?"

"I—I—suppose—Oh!" And then Dora broke from Dick's hold, as Fred Garrison and Hans Mueller appeared, around a bend of the pathway.

"Breakfast is waiting!" sang out Fred. "Hurry up, if we are to start that search."

"All right," answered Dick.—"We'll be in right away."

"See, I vos bick me a peautiful roses," put in Hans Mueller, coming closer. "Dick, of you ton't peen—vot you call him?—jealousness, yah, I gif him to Dora," and he passed over the flower.

"Oh, thank you, Hans," replied Dora, and she placed the flower in her hair. Then she gave Dick a look that meant a good deal, and they understood each other perfectly, and both went in to breakfast feeling very happy.

In the meantime Sam and Tom had been out on a side veranda with Grace and Nellie. Tom was as full of fun as ever and kept the two girls in a roar of laughter. Yet both girls grew serious when the time for parting came.

"You look out for yourself," said Grace. "Remember, those men are bad characters to meet."

"Yes, I shouldn't want you to get hurt for the world," added Nellie, and when she shook hands with Tom there was something like a tear in her eye.

Then came good-byes all around, and the carriage that was to take Dick and the others to the town drove around to the door. The party climbed in and in a moment more were off, the girls and ladies waving their handkerchiefs and the boys swinging their caps and hats.

"Yo' boys dun take good care ob yo'selves," said Aleck, who stood by, with a look of concern on his ebony face. "If yo' come back killed dis coon will neber fo'give himself!"

"Come back as soon as you can!" called out Dora.

"Don't worry—we may be back in a day or two," answered Dick. But it was destined to be many a long day ere the two parties should meet again.

Down at the riverside they found the launch in charge of a negro and all ready for the start. The provisions were stored in two lockers on board, and another locker held their firearms and some raincoats.

"Hurrah! Here is news," cried Dick, after perusing a telegram that had been handed to him. "You'll remember I telegraphed to Benton, the town below here. Well, here is word that the houseboat was seen passing Benton yesterday at about five o'clock, and headed towards the west shore. That ought to give us something to work on."

"It will," answered Harold Bird. "Come, the sooner we get started the better."

All stepped aboard of the Venus, as the launch was named, and soon the gasoline motor was buzzing away at a good rate of speed. Then the power was turned on the screw, Harold Bird took his station at the wheel, and away they sped from the landing and out onto the broad Mississippi.

"Hurrah for a life on der oceans vafe und a ship on der rollings deeps!" sang out Hans, who sat near the bow.

"Gosh, Hans is getting poetic!" said Tom. "That's right, Hansy, my boy, keep it up and you'll soon put Songbird out of business."

"What I want to know is," came from Fred, "if we strike a sunken snag is this launch safe?"

"As safe as any craft of her size," answered Harold Bird. "But I shan't strike a snag if I can help it. I am not running at full speed, and if you'll notice I am keeping where the water is fairly clear."

"Which isn't saying a great deal," came from Sam. "I never saw a river as muddy as the Mississippi."

"I know one other stream that is worse, and that's the Missouri," said Harold Bird. "And as that flows into the Mississippi it makes the latter almost as bad."

As soon as they were well on their way Dick brought out the firearms which had been brought along, and examined them with care.

"You certainly have some fine weapons," said he, referring to the pistols brought by Harold Bird. "Do you do much shooting—I mean with a gun?"

"I never go shooting at all," was the young Southerner's reply, and once again the boys saw that strange look of sadness come over his face.

"Funny, you wouldn't care to go out," said Songbird, carelessly. "Must be quite some game around here."

"There is plenty of game, but—" Harold Bird heaved a deep sigh. "I presume I may as well tell you my story, for you are bound to hear it sooner or later," he went on. "About four years ago my father went out hunting in the forest to the north of our plantation. He was out with two friends, but about the middle of the day the party separated and my father found himself alone. Then he saw something that to him looked like a wildcat on a big rock. He fired quickly, and when he drew closer he saw to his horror that he had shot and killed a man—an old hunter named Blazen.

"The shock of the discovery made my father faint, and when the others came up they found him working over the dead body of Blazen in a vain endeavor to bring the hunter back to life. A doctor was called, but nothing could be done for Blazen, for the shot had killed him instantly, taking him squarely in the heart. Of course it was an accident, but my father couldn't get over it. He raved and wept by turns, and at last the doctors had to place him in confinement for fear that he would try to do himself some injury. My mother was prostrated by the news, and you can imagine how I felt myself."

"It was certainly terrible," said Dick, and the others nodded in silence.

"Blazen was an old bachelor, with no relatives, so there were few to mourn over his death. We saw to it that he was given a decent burial and advertised for his heirs, but nobody appeared. In the meantime my father grew melancholy and the doctors thought he might become insane. They advised a trip to new scenes, and my mother and I took him to Europe and then to Kingston, Jamaica, where an old friend of the family had a plantation. One day my father disappeared."

"Disappeared?" echoed Sam and Tom.

"Yes, disappeared utterly and forever. We hunted high and low for him and offered a big reward for any information. It was useless. We have never seen him or heard a word of him since."

"And what do you think became of him?" questioned Songbird Powell.

"I cannot imagine, excepting that he may have thrown himself into the bay and drowned himself. He had a habit of going down to the water and gazing out to sea by the hour."

"Too bad!" murmured Dick. "Mr. Bird, I sympathize deeply with you."

"And so do I," came from the other boys.

"The disappearance of my father made my mother ill and it was all I could do to get her back home. There we procured the best of medical skill, but it did little good. She had always had heart trouble and this grew rapidly worse until she died, leaving me utterly alone in the world."

Harold Bird stopped speaking and wiped the tears from his eyes. All of his listeners were deeply affected. It was several seconds before anybody spoke.

"I don't wonder you don't care to go hunting," said Sam. "I'd feel the same way."

"I have never visited the forest since the time the tragedy took place," answered Harold Bird. "At first I thought to sell off the stretch of land to a lumber company, but now I have changed my mind, and I intend to give it to the heirs of Blazen, if any appear."

"Is it a valuable tract?" asked Fred.

"The lumber company offered me twenty thousand dollars for it."

"If your father was drowned it is queer that you never heard anything of his body," said Fred.

"Bodies of drowned people are not always recovered," answered the young Southerner. "But he must have been drowned, for if he had been alive we surely would have heard something of him. The reward we offered set hundreds of people to hunting for him."

"It is certainly a mystery," said Dick. "I suppose you'd give a good deal to have it cleared up.

"I'd give half of what I am worth," answered Harold Bird, earnestly.

CHAPTER V

STUCK IN THE MUD

Noon found our friends at the town of Benton—a place of some importance in the cotton trade. Without delay Dick sought out the man who had had to do with the telegrams.

"I can't tell you much more than what I put in the message," said the man. "I saw the houseboat out yonder and headed in that direction. I was watching her when a fog came up and hid her from view."

"I think I can follow her," put in Harold Bird. "Anyway, we can try."

"Did those fellows steal the houseboat?" questioned the Benton man.

"They did."

"Then I hope you catch them."

Our friends did not stop to get dinner, but took their lunch on board of the Venus. The river at Benton was broad and deep and consequently Harold Bird turned on full speed, sending the launch forward with such a rush that the water often came in a shower of spray over the bow.

"I may be mistaken, but I have an idea that those rascals headed for Lake Sico," said the young Southerner. "Gasper Pold used to hang around that lake, and most likely there are men there who would aid him in disposing of whatever is on the Dora of value."

"Where is Lake Sico?" asked Sam.

"About fifteen miles from here. It is a very broad and shallow sheet of water, and is reached by a narrow and tortuous bayou all of four miles long. One end of the lake is a perfect wilderness of bushes and brake—an ideal hiding-place for the houseboat."

"Then perhaps we had better explore the lake," said Tom.

"There is only one objection," answered Dick. "If the houseboat is not there, we'll be losing a lot of valuable time."

"Is the entrance to the bayou very narrow?" asked Tom. "For if it is, the houseboat would be apt to strike the mud shore and leave marks."

"Yes, it is narrow, and we'll look for marks by all means," answered the young Southerner.

As they were moving with the stream it did not take the launch long to reach the bayou that connected the lake with the Mississippi. But close to the bayou entrance the swirling waters had cast up a ridge or bar of mud and on this the launch slid and stuck fast.

"Hullo, we're stuck!" cried Tom.

"And we are up out of the water too," came from his younger brother.

"Can't we back?" asked Fred.

"I'll try it," returned Harold Bird.

The screw of the launch was reversible and he made the change in power. The water was churned up into a muddy foam, but that was all. The Venus did not budge an inch.

"One of the joys of a life 'on der rollings deeps'!" grumbled Tom, imitating Hans. "Songbird, can't you compose an ode in honor of the occasion?"

"Certainly I can," said Songbird promptly, and started:

> "As firm as a rock, our launch now rests
> Upon her bed of mud,
> As safe as a ship on a golden sea—"

"Or a clothespin in a tub!"

finished Tom. "Songbird, give us something better, or none at all."

"Say, vot has a clothesbin in a dub to do mit being stuck here alretty?" questioned Hans, innocently.

"Why, Hansy, old boy, that's easy," cried Tom. "A clothespin is for sticking something fast, and we are stuck fast. Now, can't you see the joke, as the blind astronomer said to the deaf musician?"

"Yah, dot's so, but ve ain't stuck on no clothes-pins," answered Hans, soberly. "Ve vos stuck on der Mississippies Rifer, ain't it."

"Score one for Hans," came, with a laugh, from Sam. "Hans, what do you think we ought to do?"

"Dake a rope py der shore und bull der poat loose."

"That's the talk," said Songbird. "Hans can carry the rope ashore. The water is only a foot deep."

"And the mud is about sixteen feet deep," put in Dick, quickly. "Don't try it, unless you want to sink out of sight."

For several minutes all sat still in the launch, viewing the situation with considerable dismay.

"This is something I didn't bargain for," said Fred. "But we may as well make the best of it."

"Let us try to shove her off," suggested Dick.

On board the launch were three poles of good size, each fixed so that a small, square board could be fastened to one end. Dick took one of these poles and Tom and Sam seized the others.

"Now, Hans, Fred, and Songbird, get in the stern," said Dick.

"That's the talk, and I'll try to back her at the same time!" cried Harold Bird. "All ready?"

In a minute they were ready to try the experiment and the power was turned on. As the screw churned the water and mud once more, the three Rovers pushed on the poles with all their might.

"Hurrah! she's moving!" cried Fred.

He was right, the Venus was slowly but surely leaving the bank of mud. Suddenly she gave a twist and then ran backwards rapidly, and then the power was shut off again.

"Free at last!" cried Tom. "Now what's the next move?"

"We must find the proper channel into the bayou," answered the owner of the launch.

Dick and Tom went to the front with their poles and the power was turned to a slow speed forward. The Rovers felt their way in the water with the poles, calling to turn to the right or the left, as the case required. By this means they soon left the treacherous mud bars behind and reached a point where forward progress was more certain.

"Now then, let us look around and see if we can find any traces of the Dora," said Dick.

"The houseboat couldn't have come over that spot—she would have been stuck sure," said Fred.

"Years ago Solly Jackson used to be a riverman," said Harold Bird. "He would probably know exactly how to get the houseboat into the bayou. Gasper Pold couldn't run the craft himself, so he had to take in a fellow like Solly."

As the gasoline launch entered the bayou all kept their eyes on the alert, and presently Songbird set up a shout:

"Look over yonder—there are some sort of marks on the bank!"

He was right, and they turned the launch in the direction indicated, advancing slowly. There was a sharp cut in the mud and also several pole holes which looked to be rather fresh. A few feet further on they came to a piece of a pole painted blue.

"That settles it," exclaimed Dick. "They certainly brought the houseboat in here. Our poles were painted blue, and that is a piece of one."

"The very one I cracked in the storm," added Sam.

"I can explain it," said Harold Bird. "They got the houseboat around the mud bars, but the force of the current, combined with the current in the bayou, swung the craft up against this bank. Then they had to pole the houseboat off."

"But how did they go on, against the current from the lake?" asked Songbird.

"Pulled and poled the houseboat. Just wait and see if I am not right."

They waited, and soon reached a point where one bank of the bayou was fairly firm. Here they could see footprints and the "shaving" of a rope as it had passed over the edge of the bank.

"We are on the right track," said Dick. "Now, all we have to do is to locate the houseboat and corner the rascals who stole her."

"All!" cried Fred. "I should say that was enough!"

"Especially if they offer to fight," added Sam.

"It is a pity we can't come on them unawares," said Tom. "But that is impossible, for you can't run the launch without making a noise."

"Maybe you don't besser git out dem bistols alretty," came from Hans. "Of da ton't gif ub ve plow der heads off, ain't it!"

"Yes, we may as well get out the firearms," said Dick. "The sight of the pistols may have a good effect. Perhaps the rascals will give up without fighting."

The pistols were gotten out, and all of the youths saw to it that they were in perfect condition for immediate use. As he looked at the weapons Harold Bird shuddered.

"I suppose you hate the sight of them,—after what happened to your father," said Dick, in a low tone.

"I do. I sincerely trust there is no bloodshed," answered the young Southerner.

It was nightfall by the time the launch was clear of the bayou. In front of them lay the calm waters of Lake Sico—a shallow expanse, with mud flats at one side and a wilderness of trees, bushes, and wild canebrake at the other. They shut off the power and listened. Not a sound broke the stillness.

"Talk about solitude," was Tom's comment. "Here is where you can chop it out with an ax!"

"It's enough to make one shiver," added Fred.

Just then the dog Harold Bird had brought along set up a mournful howl.

"Even the dog doesn't like it," said Songbird. "Let us go on—I'd rather hear the puff-puff of the gasoline motor than listen to such stillness."

"I thought a poet craved solitude," said Dick. "This ought to fill you with inspiration."

"I think it will fill us with chills and fever," said Fred. "Ugh, how damp it is, now the sun is going down."

"There is a mist creeping up," said Harold Bird. "Too bad! I was in hope it would remain clear."

Soon the darkness of night settled over the lake. The mist continued to roll over them until they were completely enveloped and could no longer see where they were going.

"It can't be helped," said the owner of the launch. "We'll have to wait until daylight. If I light the acetylene gas lamp it will simply put those rascals on guard."

"Vot is ve going to do—sthay on der poat all night?" asked Hans.

"We can either do that or go ashore—just as you wish."

"Let us move towards shore," said Dick. "It will be more pleasant under some overhanging trees or bushes."

This was agreed to, and they steered for the bank of the lake, which was not far away. None of them dreamed of what that night was to bring forth.

CHAPTER VI

FIGHTING BOB CATS

It was certainly a dismal and dreary outlook, and it did not help matters much to run the launch under the wide overhanging boughs of several trees growing at the edge of the lake. They were in something of a cove, so the view was shut off on three sides.

"I wish we had brought along some extra blankets," said Sam. "If it is raw now what will it be by midnight?"

"Hadn't we better build a little campfire?" questioned Fred. "It will make it ever so much more pleasant."

"I do not advise a fire," answered Harold Bird. "If those rascals should see it, they'd come here to investigate, and then try to slip away from us in the darkness."

"You are right," put in Dick. "We must keep dark until we have located them,—otherwise the game will be up."

To protect themselves still more from the mist and cold, they brought out four rubber blankets of good size. These were laced into one big sheet and raised over the launch like an awning. Then all huddled beneath, to make themselves as comfortable as possible.

"Don't you think somebody ought to remain on guard?" asked Tom. "We don't want those fellows to carry us off and us not know it!"

"Da can't vos carry me off dot vay," said Hans, who could never see the funny side of a remark. "I vould kick, I tole you!"

"As there are seven of us, why not have everybody stand guard for just an hour?" suggested Sam. "If we turn in at ten that will carry us through to five in the morning—when we ought to continue our hunt."

"Providing the mist will let us," smiled Harold Bird. "But I think your plan a good one," he added.

Lots were drawn and Fred went on guard first, to be followed by Hans and Tom. At ten o'clock all of the crowd but Fred turned in, to get as much sleep as possible.

"I tole you vot." remarked Hans, as he tried to make his head feel easy on one of the seats. "Dis ton't vos so goot like mine ped at Putnam Hall!"

"Not by a good deal!" answered Songbird. "Dear old Putnam Hall! After all the pleasures we have had, I shall be glad to get back to that institution again."

The Rover boys had been through so much excitement during their lives they did not think the present situation unusual and so all went to sleep without an effort. Harold Bird remained awake nearly an hour, thinking of the new friends he had made and of the strange fate of his father. The young Southerner was of a somewhat retiring disposition, and it astonished even himself when he realized how he had opened his heart to the Rovers and their chums.

"I feel as if I had known them for years, instead of hours," he told himself. "There is a certain attractiveness about Sam, Tom, and Dick I cannot understand. Yet I do not wonder that they have a host of friends who are willing to do almost anything for them."

When Tom went on guard he was still sleepy and he did a large amount of yawning before he could get himself wide-awake. He sat up in the bow of the launch, the others resting on the cushions on the sides and stern. All was as silent as a tomb, and the mist was now so thick that he could not see a distance of six yards in any direction.

"Ugh! what a disagreeable night!" he muttered, as he gave a shiver. "I'd give as much as a toothpick and a bottle of hair-oil if it was morning and the sun was shining."

A quarter of an hour went by—to Tom it seemed ten times as long as that—and then of a sudden the lad heard a movement at the bottom of the launch. The dog Harold Bird had brought along arose, stretched himself, and listened intently.

"What is it, Dandy?" asked Tom, patting the animal on the head. "What do you hear?"

For reply the dog continued to listen. Then the hair on his back began to rise and he set up a short, sharp bark.

"He certainly hears something," reasoned Tom. "Can any of those men be in this vicinity?"

The bow of the launch was close to a sprawling tree branch, and to look beyond the rubber covering, Tom crawled forward and stepped on the branch. The dog followed to the extreme bow of the boat and gave another short, sharp bark.

"He hears something, that is certain," mused the boy. "But what it can be, is a puzzle to me."

Tom tried to pierce the darkness and mist, but it was impossible. He strained his ears, but all he could hear was the occasional dropping of water from one leaf to another over his head.

"Maybe I had better arouse the others," he murmured, for the barking of the dog had apparently not disturbed them. "I am sure the dog wouldn't bark unless there was a reason for it; would you, Dandy?"

Tom looked at the animal and saw the dog had his nose pointed up in the tree next to that which the launch was under. He peered in the direction and gave a start.

Was he mistaken, or had he caught the glare of a pair of shining eyes fastened upon him? Tom was naturally a brave boy, yet a strange shiver took possession of him. The dog now bristled furiously and gave two sharp barks in quick succession.

"Hullo, what's up?" came from Dick, who was awakened.

"I believe there is some wild animal up yonder tree, spotting us," answered Tom. "I think I just caught a glimpse of its eyes."

This announcement caused Dick to rouse up, and taking his pistol he crawled to the bow of the launch and joined his brother on the tree limb. Just then the dog started to bark furiously.

"There he is!" cried Tom, and raised the pistol he had in his pocket. There could be no mistake about those glaring eyes, and taking hasty aim, he fired.

The report of the firearm had not yet died away when there came the wild and unmistakable screech of a wounded bob cat—a wildcat well known in certain portions of our southern states. At the same time the dog began to bark furiously, and everybody on board the launch was aroused.

"What's the matter?"

"Who fired that shot?"

"Vos dose rascals here to fight mit us alretty?"

"It's a bob cat!" cried Dick. "Tom just fired at it!"

"Look out, it's coming down!" yelled Tom, and that instant the bob cat, unable to support itself longer on the tree limb, fell with a snarl on the rubber covering of the launch, carrying it down upon those underneath.

The next few minutes things happened so rapidly that it is almost impossible to describe them. The bob cat rolled over and over, clawing at the rubber cloth and ripping it to shreds. The boys tried to get another shot, but did not dare to fire for fear of hitting each other. But the dog leaped in and caught the bob cat by the back of the neck, and an instant later cat and canine went whirling over the side of the boat into the waters of the lake.

"They are overboard!" cried Sam.

"Make a light, somebody!" yelled Songbird. "It isn't safe in the dark."

The acetylene gas lamp of the launch was ready for use, and striking a match Harold Bird lit it. The sharp rays were turned on the water, and there dog and bob cat could be seen whirling around in a mad struggle for supremacy.

Bang! went Dick's pistol. He had taken quick but accurate aim, and the bob cat was hit in the side. It went under with a yelp, letting go of the dog as it did so. Dandy gave a final nip and then turned and swam back to the launch and was helped aboard by his master.

AND THERE DOG AND BOB CAT COULD BE SEEN WHIRLING
AROUND IN A MAD STRUGGLE.

"Wonder if the bob cat is dead?" asked Fred, in a voice that he tried in vain to steady.

"Hasn't come up again," came laconically from Songbird. He had taken the lamp from Harold Bird and was sending the rays over the surface of the lake in several directions.

They watched for several minutes and then made out the dead form of the bob cat floating among the bushes on the opposite side of the little cove.

"Done for—and I am glad of it," murmured Tom, and he wiped the cold perspiration from his forehead.

"I don't know if we are out of the woods or not," said the owner of the launch. "Where there is one bob cat there are often more."

"In that case I think we had better move the boat away from the shore," answered Dick. "It may not be as comfortable as under the trees but it will be safer."

At that moment the gas lamp began to flicker and die down.

"Here, give the lamp to me," said the launch owner, and taking the lamp he shook it and tried to turn more water on the carbide. But the water would not run for some reason and a few seconds later the light went out.

In the darkness the boys started to untie the launch. As they did this they heard a movement in the tree directly over their heads and then came the cry of a bob cat calling its mate.

"There's another!" yelled Sam. "Say, we had better get out as fast as we can!"

The gasoline launch was just shoved away from the tree limb when the bob cat above made a leap and landed on the bow of the craft! It glared a moment at the boys, its two eyes shining like balls of fire, and then started to make a leap.

Bang! crack! bang! went three pistols in rapid succession, and as the reports died away the bob cat fell in a heap on the bottom of the launch, snarling viciously. Then Dandy, still exhausted from his fight in the water, leaped on the beast and held it down while Tom finished it with a bullet in the ear.

"Is it dead?" asked Songbird, after a painful silence.

"I guess so. Light a match, somebody."

Several matches were lit and then an old oil lantern which chanced to be on board. The bob cat was indeed dead and near it lay the dog, with a deep scratch in its foreshoulder.

"Noble Dandy, you did what you could," said Harold Bird, affectionately.

Very gingerly Tom and Dick picked up the carcass of the bob cat and threw it overboard. By this time the launch had drifted a good fifty feet from shore, and there they anchored.

"Keep that lantern lit," said Fred. "I can't stand the darkness after such doings!"

"If those thieves are around they must have heard the shots," said Sam. "So a light won't make much difference."

"I am going to examine the gas lamp," said the young Southerner, and did so. A bit of dirt had gotten into the feed pipe of the lamp, and when this was cleaned out with a thin wire the light worked as well as ever.

It was some time after the excitement before any of the crowd could get to sleep again. Then Hans got a nightmare and yelled "Bop cats! fire! murder!" and other things as loudly as he could, and that put further rest out of the question, and all waited anxiously for the coming of morning.

CHAPTER VII

THE HOUSEBOAT IN THE BUSHES

With the coming of morning the mist cleared away as if by magic, and soon the warm sunshine put all on board of the gasoline launch in better spirits.

"How is the dog?" questioned Dick, of the owner of the canine.

"He has been pretty well mauled up, but I think he'll come around with proper attention," answered the young Southerner. "He is a valuable animal—valuable to me because he was a pet of my father—and I'd hate to lose him."

All were hungry and ate their morning lunch with considerable satisfaction, washing it down with some coffee made on a small oil stove that had been brought along.

"Well, I don't see anything of the houseboat," announced Dick, as he stood on a seat and took a long and careful look around. "Not a craft or a building of any kind in sight."

"Some negroes used to live on the north shore of the lake," said Harold Bird, "but the floods last year made them vacate in a hurry."

It was decided to move around the shore of the lake slowly, scanning every cove and inlet with care. That the houseboat was hidden somewhere on that expanse of water none of the party had any doubt.

"You could take quite a trip in this launch," said Sam to Harold Bird, as they moved along. "The more I see of the craft the better I like her. May I ask what she is worth?"

"I gave two thousand dollars for her. I bought her in New Orleans and brought her up the river myself. The folks around here don't know much about gasoline launches, but I think she's as nice a craft as anybody would wish."

"How much water does she draw?"

"Only two and a half feet when loaded down—so you see we can get over some pretty shallow spots, if it is necessary."

They were moving along a scantily-wooded stretch of shore when Tom let out a short cry:

"Stop!"

"What's up, Tom?" asked several.

"I saw somebody just now—back of yonder bushes. He stepped out and then stepped back again."

"Was it one of the men we are after?" asked Sam.

"I don't know—he got out of sight before I had a good look at him."

"We'll have to investigate," said Dick, and to this the others agreed. With all possible haste the launch was run to the shore and Sam, Tom, and Dick got out, followed by Harold Bird. The dog came also, limping along painfully.

"Find him, Dandy, find him!" said the young Southerner, in a low tone, and the dog seemed to understand. He put his nose to the ground, ran around for several minutes, and then started off through the bushes.

"Do you think he has struck the trail?" asked Tom.

"I am sure of it," was Harold Bird's positive reply.

The young Southerner called to the dog, and Dandy went forward more slowly, so that they could keep him in sight. They passed through one patch of bushes and then came to a clear space, beyond which was a field of wild sugarcane.

Hardly had the dog struck the cleared spot when from a distance came the report of a pistol. Dandy leaped up in the air, came down in a heap, and lay still.

"Somebody has shot the dog!" cried Sam. "What a shame!"

Harold Bird said nothing, but ran to where the canine lay. Dandy was breathing his last, and in a minute it was all over.

"Poor fellow!" murmured the young Southerner, and there were tears in his eyes. "First the bob cats and now a pistol bullet! Oh, if I can only catch the rascal who fired that shot I'll make him suffer for this!"

"The fellow killed the dog, so the animal could not trail him," said Dick. "It was certainly a dirty trick."

"It shows that the man is a criminal," put in Tom. "He would not be afraid of us if he was honest."

"And therefore it must have been Gasper Pold or Solly Jackson," said Sam.

"What will you do with the dog?" asked Dick, after an awkward pause.

"Take him back to the boat and bury him," answered the young Southerner. "I don't want the wild beasts to feed on him."

"Hadn't we better follow up that man first?"

"We can do so, if you wish."

They passed on and looked around that vicinity with care. It must be confessed that they were afraid of being shot at, but nothing of the sort occurred. At one point they saw some footsteps, but these came to an end in a creek flowing into the lake.

As the ground in that vicinity was very treacherous there was nothing to do but to return to the launch and this they did, Harold Bird and Dick carrying the dead dog between them. All were sorry that the canine was dead, for they realized that the animal had done its best for them against the bob cats.

They had no spade, but with some flat sticks managed to scoop out a hole of respectable depth and in this they buried the canine. Over the spot the young Southerner placed a peculiar stick to mark the spot.

"He was a fine dog and was once the pet of my father," he said. "Some day I may place a monument over his grave."

They left the vicinity and continued on their trip around the lake, scanning every indentation of the shore for a possible glimpse of the Dora. There were many winding places, so it was noon before the task was half completed.

"This is growing to be a longer hunt than I anticipated," remarked Fred. "I thought finding the houseboat would be dead easy."

Lunch was had, and once again they went on the search, this time at a point where a bayou joined Lake Sico to a smaller lake. Here they had to move with care, for the bayou was filled with the hidden roots of trees long since thrown down by storms.

"Of ve ton't look out ve peen caught in dem dree roots," observed Hans, looking down into the water. "Say, ton't da look like vater snakes?"

"They certainly do, and they are almost as dangerous—for the launch."

Soon came a grinding tinder the boat and the screw came to a standstill. A tree root had caught fast, and further progress was out of the question until the screw could be cleared.

"I'll go over and do the job!" cried Tom. "I know how." And the others being willing he divested himself of most of his clothing, leaped overboard, and was soon at work. It was no light task, as he had to cut the root in several places with a jackknife.

"We had better land and look around," said Harold Bird. "I'd hate to get the screw caught again and break it, for then we'd certainly be in a pickle."

"Could the houseboat get through here?" questioned Fred.

"Yes, they could pole her through, with hard work," answered Dick.

They turned the gasoline launch to shore and tied fast. Then all began to leap out.

"This won't do," cried Dick. "Somebody ought to remain on the launch."

"I would like to go with you and look for the houseboat," answered Harold Bird. "I think the launch will be safe where she is."

"If you want me to stay I'll do it, if Songbird will stay with me," said Fred.

"I'll stay," said Songbird, promptly.

So it was arranged, and leaving the two in charge of the gasoline launch, all the others of the party set off on their search for the missing houseboat.

Walking along the shore of the small lake was decidedly treacherous, and more than once one or another would slip down in the mud and slime.

"Hellup!" cried Hans, who had dragged behind, and looking back they saw the German lad in a bog hole up to his knees. "Hellup, oder I vos trowned alretty!"

"Can't you crawl out?" questioned Dick, running back.

"No, der mud vos like glue!" gasped Hans.

Tom came back also, and between them they managed to pull Hans from the sticky ooze, which was plastered over his trousers and shoes. The German lad gazed at himself ruefully.

"Now, ain't dot a nice mess?" he observed. "Vosn't I a beach!"

"Yes, but a pretty muddy one," laughed Dick. "But never mind now, come on. You can clean up when we get back."

The party soon reached a spot where the bushes grew in water several inches deep. Here, to avoid sinking in the mud, they had to make a wide detour.

"Listen!" cried Sam, presently, and held up his hand.

"What did you hear?" asked Harold Bird.

"I heard something as if somebody was walking through the brush yonder!"

"Maybe it was the men we are after!" cried Dick. "Come on!"

They continued to move forward until some fallen trees all but barred their further progress. Then they came to a small rise of ground—a veritable island in this swamp,—and reaching the highest point, gazed around them.

"What is that?" asked Sam, pointing with his hand to a round, black object showing above some bushes at a distance.

"Why, that looks like the smokestack of the houseboat!" cried Tom. He meant the stack to the chimney, for several rooms of the houseboat were furnished with stoves, to be used when the weather was chilly.

"We'll soon make certain," said Dick. "Forward, everybody!"

"Be careful!" cautioned Harold Bird. "Remember, you have desperate characters with whom to deal."

"Isn't everybody armed?" asked Sam. "I brought my pistol."

All were armed, and each took out his weapon and carried it in his hand. They wanted no shooting, but, after the killing of the dog, decided to take no chances.

It was no light task to reach the spot where the smokestack had been seen. They had another creek to cross and then had to crawl through some extra-thick bushes. But beyond was a stretch of clear water, and there they saw, safely tied to two trees, the object of their search, the missing houseboat.

CHAPTER VIII

IN THE SWAMP

"There she is!"

"She seems to be all right!"

"Shall we go on board?"

Such were the cries from the Rovers and their friends as they came in sight of the Dora. The view of the houseboat filled them all with pleasure.

"Wait!" said Harold Bird. "Don't show yourselves!"

Dick at least understood and held the others back.

"Keep out of sight—we want to investigate first," he said, in a low tone. "There is no use in our running our heads into the lion's mouth."

"Mine cracious, vos der a lion aroundt here?" demanded Hans, turning pale.

"Maybe you'll find a lion if you don't keep quiet," answered Sam, with a snicker.

After that but little was said. Gradually they drew so close that they could see from one end of the Dora to the other. Not a person was in sight.

"Really does look as if the craft was deserted," was Harold Bird's comment. "Perhaps they got scared when they saw what a crowd was following them."

"I move two of us go on board and the rest stay here," said Tom. "Then, if there is trouble, the crowd to stay behind can come to the rescue."

"That's a good scheme," answered his elder brother. "Supposing Sam and I go? You can lead the rescuing party, if it becomes necessary."

This was also agreed to, and a minute later Dick and Sam, with their pistols in hand, crawled from the bushes and made for the side of the houseboat. A gangplank was out and they saw the footprints of several men and also two horses.

"I don't like those much," said Dick, pointing to the hoofprints. "A horse here means that he was used for carrying some stuff away."

As nobody came to stop them, they walked on board of the Dora and looked into the gallery, that being the nearest apartment. The cook stove was still there, just as Aleck Pop had left it, but the pots and kettles were scattered in all directions and some of the best of the utensils were missing.

"This looks as if the houseboat had been looted!" cried Dick, and ran from the galley to the dining room and then to the living room, while Sam made his way to several of the staterooms.

Nobody but themselves was on board the houseboat and they soon announced that fact to the others in the bushes, and they came forward on a run.

"Did they steal anything?" demanded Tom.

"Steal anything?" repeated Sam. "They have taken about everything they could lay their hands on!"

"Everything is gone but the stove, piano, and bedding," said Dick. "And just to show their meanness they hacked the top of the piano with a hatchet!"

What Dick said was almost wholly true. The rascals had stolen everything of value that they could possibly carry, leaving behind little outside of the things already mentioned. Not only was the piano mutilated, but also the chairs, the dining-room table, and the berths in the stateroom. All of the lanterns but one were missing, and the small rowboat resting on the rear deck of the houseboat had its side stove in from an ax-blow.

"The fiends!" muttered Dick, as he gazed at the wreckage. "What they couldn't carry they tried to ruin!"

"What could you expect from fellows who would shoot my pet dog?" returned Harold Bird.

"I tell you, Dick Rover, those men ought to be landed in jail!"

"Well, we'll land them there!" cried Dick, earnestly.

"Do you mean that?"

"I certainly do."

"I will aid you all I can," answered the young Southerner heartily.

After that all made a thorough examination of the houseboat, to learn if they could find out anything concerning the thieves. Muddy footprints were visible in every apartment, but they told little.

"I think we are simply wasting time here," said Tom, presently. "The best we can do is to follow up those footprints outside and see where they lead to."

"Dot's so," said Hans. "Dis muss is so bad like it vill pe Lund vill get no petter py looking at him, ain't dot so?"

"All right, come on," said Sam, and led the way off the houseboat. "I don't believe those chaps intend to come back. They took all they wanted."

To follow the footprints was no easy task, and before long, they found themselves going through a swamp where the walking was extremely treacherous.

"I don't like this," said Sam. "They may have known the way, but we don't; and if we don't look out we'll get in so deep we'll be helpless."

"Yah, let us go back," said Hans, who had not forgotten his experience in the bog hole. "A feller can't schwim in vater mit mud up to his neck alretty!"

Again they had to turn back. As they did this Dick fancied he heard a faraway cry for help.

"Did you hear that?" he asked of Tom. "What?"

"I heard somebody call, I think."

"So did I," put in Harold Bird. "Listen!"

They listened, but the cry, or whatever it was, was not repeated. Soon they were back to the side of the houseboat once more.

"Do you think that call came from Fred or Songbird?" asked Sam.

"It might be, Sam," answered Dick. "Maybe we had better get back to the launch."

"Yes, yes, let us go back by all means!" exclaimed Harold Bird. "If your friends are in trouble we ought to aid them."

As rapidly as they could do so, they started back for the spot where the gasoline launch had been left. Once they lost their way, and got into a swamp from which it was next to impossible to get out.

"We'll have to go back!" cried Sam, after he had moved in several directions, only to find himself worse off than before.

"Be careful," warned Harold Bird. "If you aren't careful—Stop!"

All of the boys halted, for the command was out of the ordinary. The young Southerner was looking straight ahead of him.

"What is it?" questioned Tom, in a low tone, thinking some of the enemy might be near.

"Am I right, and is that a snake ahead?" asked Harold Bird. "It looks like a snake and still it may be nothing but the dead limb of a tree."

"Say, I ton't vonts me no snakes in mine!" ejaculated Hans, trying to retreat.

All the boys gazed at the object ahead with interest. Then Tom broke off a stick near him and threw it at the object. The latter did not budge.

"Must be a tree limb," said Tom. "But it looked enough like a snake to frighten anybody."

"I am not sure yet," answered Harold Bird. "You must remember that some of our southern snakes are very sluggish and only move when they are hungry or harassed."

"We'll give the limb, or whatever it is, a wide berth," said Sam.

They started to move to one side. But Tom was curious, and chancing to see a stone among some bushes, hurled it at the object, hitting it directly in the center.

Up came an ugly-looking head, the object whipped around

swiftly, and the next instant the boys found themselves confronted by a swamp snake all of six feet long and as thick as a man's wrist!

"Mine cracious!" burst from Hans' lips. "It vos a snake annahow! Look out! he vill eat us up alife!"

"We must get out of here!" cried Sam. "Oh, Tom, why didn't you leave it alone?"

"I didn't really think it was a snake," answered the fun-loving Rover. "Somebody shoot it!"

Queer as it was, nobody had thought to use his pistol, but as Tom spoke Dick pointed his weapon at the snake, that was crawling rapidly over the tree roots towards them. The puff of smoke was followed by a writhing of the reptile, and they saw that it had been hit although not fatally wounded.

"Wait, I'll give him another shot!" cried Sam, who now had his pistol out, and as the head of the snake came up over a tree root, the youngest Rover fired point-blank. His aim was true, and the head of the snake went down, and the body whirled this way and that in its death agonies.

"Is he—he dead?" faltered Tom.

"Next door to it," answered Harold Bird. "That last shot took him directly in the throat. I do not think he will bother us any more."

They saw the body of the snake sink down in the water beneath the upper roots of the tree, and then continued to retreat, making their way to what looked like safer ground. They were now completely turned around, with only the sun to guide them in their course.

"This is no joke," said Dick, gazing around in perplexity. "If we are not careful we'll become hopelessly lost."

"I think somebody had better climb a tree and look around," said Tom. "I'll go up if somebody will boost me."

The others were willing, and soon the fun-loving youth was climbing a tall tree which stood somewhat apart from the others. He went up in rapid fashion and before long was close to the top.

"Can you see anything?" called up Sam, after what seemed to be a long pause.

"Hello!" cried Tom. "Why, there is the small lake and, yes, the launch is moving from the shore."

"The launch?" ejaculated Harold Bird. "Do you mean my gasoline launch?"

"It must be yours—or some craft very much like it," answered Tom. "There, it is out of sight now behind the trees."

Tom waited for fully a minute, but the launch did not reappear.

"Who was on board?" questioned Dick, as his brother came down.

"I couldn't make out."

"Which is the way to the spot where we tied up?" asked the young Southerner, impatiently. "We must investigate this without delay."

"Over that way," answered Tom, pointing the direction out with his hand. "Come, I think I saw a good way to go."

Then all of the party struck out to reach the landing-place without delay. They felt that something unusual had occurred, but what, they could not surmise.

CHAPTER IX

TWO YOUNG PRISONERS

Left to themselves. Fred Garrison and Songbird Powell hardly knew what to do to pass away the time. With all of the others away the spot where the gasoline launch had been tied up appeared to be unusually lonely.

"I can tell you what, I shouldn't care to be caught all alone at night in such a spot as this," said Fred, with something of a shiver. "It is about as dismal as any place I've seen."

"Right you are," murmured Songbird and then continued:

"The lonely waters washed the lonely shore,
Where they had washed full many a moon before,
I listened pensively—not a sound
Was there to break the tomblike silence all around!"

"Great mackerel, Songbird!" cried Fred. "Don't go on like that. It's enough to give a fellow the creeps!" But the would-be poet only continued:

"I listened for a single bird,
But not a note my ear there heard,
I looked up in the calm, clear sky—"

"And nervous enough was I to fly!"

finished Fred, and went on: "Songbird, if you've got to make up poetry give us something cheerful. Can't you make up something about—er—about circus clowns, or apple pie, or—er—"

"Circus clowns or apple pie!" snorted the would-be poet, in deep disgust. "Well, you are the limit, Fred Garrison. No, I can't make up poetry about circus pie or apple clo—I mean apple clowns or circus, pshaw, you know what I mean—"

"I didn't mention mixed pickles," observed Fred, demurely. "But if you can mix—What's that?"

He stopped short and straightened up on the launch seat, and so did Songbird. Both had heard voices at a distance.

"They must be coming back," said Songbird. "It didn't take them long."

They listened, and set up a call, but no answer came back. Then they looked around searchingly.

"That's funny," murmured Fred.

"I don't think it's funny," was the low answer. "Something is wrong."

"Help! My foot is caught!" came presently, in a muffled voice. "Hello, the launch! Help me somebody, quick!"

"Who is that calling?" asked Songbird.

"Somebody of our crowd and in trouble," answered Fred, and leaped ashore with Songbird at his heels.

The call had come from a thicket about a hundred feet away, and in that direction dashed the two unsuspecting youths, never dreaming of the plan laid to trap them. As they ran into the thicket four persons came behind them, and in a trice each was thrown violently forward on the ground and held there.

"Wha—what does this mean?" gasped Fred, as soon as he could get his breath.

"It means that you are prisoners," came in the voice of Gasper Pold. "Keep quiet now, it will be best for you."

"Blindfold 'em and be quick about it," came in a low tone from one of the others of the party.

"Dan Baxter!" exclaimed Songbird, recognizing that voice. "Is it possible! I thought you died in the swamp!"

"Hang the luck!" muttered the former bully of Putnam Hall. "I didn't want them to know I was here."

By this time the two boys had had their hands tied behind them. Then they were allowed to rise.

"Don't you make a noise, if you value your lives," came from another of the men, and to their surprise they saw that it was Sack

Todd, one of the head counterfeiters of Red Rock ranch and the only man who had escaped from the authorities at the time the noted gang was rounded up. How slick an individual this chap was those who have read "The Rover Boys on the Plains" already know.

The boys now saw that the fourth person who had attacked them and made them prisoners was the carpenter Solly Jackson. The fellow took small part in the proceedings and was apparently under the thumb of Gasper Pold.

"What is the meaning of this outrage?" asked Songbird.

"You'll find out quick enough," answered Dan Baxter, with a chuckle. "So you thought I perished in the swamp, eh? Ha! ha! I thought I'd fool you!"

"Did you get away with Sack Todd?" asked Fred.

"Not exactly—but we soon met—after that fight was over—and here we are, to fix you for interfering with our business," went on the big bully.

"Look here, Baxter, we can't stop to talk now," broke in Gasper Pold. "Those other fellows will be back soon. We've got to make the best possible use of our time."

"Tie 'em to the trees," said Sack Todd. "Quick now, and then we'll be off. You say you can run the launch?" he asked, turning to the former bully of Putnam Hall.

"Sure I can—used to do that sort of thing at home, years ago," replied Dan Baxter.

Without ceremony Fred and Songbird were tied fast to two trees near by, the ropes being passed from their wrists directly around each tree. Then the men and Baxter departed, taking with them several heavy bundles which they had been carrying.

"That stuff they have must be from the houseboat," said Fred, when he and Songbird were left alone in the forest. "They are going to run off with it on the launch!"

"I reckon you are right." Songbird gave a groan. "Gosh! they tied my wrists together so tightly the blood won't circulate!"

"They are first-class rascals, and Dan Baxter is as bad as any of them," was the answer. "Isn't it strange that he should escape from that swamp, and after losing his horse, too!"

After that the two prisoners listened intently and soon heard the putt-putt of the gasoline launch, as the power was turned on. Gradually the sound grew fainter and fainter.

"They are off!" sighed Fred. "Perhaps now we'll never see the launch again!"

"This will make Harold Bird angry, Fred. First his pet dog and now his new launch. He'll want to land those rascals in jail just as much as we do."

Half an hour went by—the young prisoners thought it must be four times that long,—and still nobody came near them. Each tried to free himself from his bonds, but without avail. Fred cut one wrist and Songbird scraped off the skin and that was all.

"It's no use," sighed the would-be poet. "We'll have to stay here till the others get back."

"What fools we were to be deceived into thinking one of our party was in trouble! I thought that cry for help didn't seem just right. We walked right into the trap."

"I was afraid—My gracious me! Look!"

At this exclamation both boys looked into the forest they were facing and there they saw a sight that almost made the blood freeze in their veins. Crouching down between some bushes was a bob cat larger than either of those that had been killed the night before.

"Oh!" cried Songbird. "Scat!"

At the cry the bob cat turned and disappeared into the bushes like a flash. But then they heard it leap into a tree, and the rustling of the branches told them only too plainly that it was approaching closer and closer.

"This is—is awful!" groaned Fred. "It will surely pounce down and tear us to pieces. Help! help, somebody! Help!"

Songbird joined in the cry and the forest rang loudly with the sounds of their voices. Then they stopped to get their breath.

"I see him—he is almost over our heads!" gasped Songbird. "Help! Help!" he yelled, at the top of his lungs.

"What's the trouble?" came from close at hand, and Dick Rover burst into view, with Tom and Sam at his heels and each with his revolver drawn. Not far behind were Hans and Harold Bird.

"A bob cat! Look out for him!" cried Fred.

"Protect us!" put in Songbird. "We are helpless!"

"See, they are tied to the trees!" exclaimed Tom. "What does this mean?"

"I see the bob cat!" said Sam Rover, and without ado fired up into the tree. Down came the beast, spitting viciously and clawing the air, to fall at Tom's feet. Bang! went Tom's pistol and then all of the others fired, and almost as quick as I can tell it the beast lay dead where it had fallen. Then the boys looked around for other bob cats, but none showed themselves.

"Oh, how thankful I am that you came," said Fred, as he was being released.

"And you didn't arrive a minute too soon either," said Songbird. "That bob cat was getting ready to spring on us! It was a narrow escape!"

"Who made you prisoners?" asked Dick. "But I suppose it was that Gasper Pold and his tools."

"Yes, and who do you think his tools are?" answered Fred.—"Solly Jackson, Sack Todd—"

"Sack Todd!" exclaimed Sam.

"Yes, and Dan Baxter."

"Baxter!" came from the others.

"The young rascal you told me about?" said Harold Bird.

"Exactly, and all of them have run away with your launch," put in Songbird. "They went quite a while ago."

"I was afraid of it," answered the young Southerner. "Of course they must have steered for Lake Sico."

"Yes, and as they have had a good start, they must be a long way off by now," added Tom.

CHAPTER X

THE CHASE ON THE RIVER

The whole party walked down to where the launch had been tied up, and Fred and Songbird told their story and then heard of what had happened to the houseboat.

"What rascals!" murmured Fred. "We must do our level best to catch them."

"I am going to catch them, if I have to follow them a thousand miles!" exclaimed Harold Bird, impulsively.

"That's the talk!" came from Dick. "We are bound to catch them sooner or later, if we stick to the chase."

Yet, though he spoke so hopefully, the outlook just then was dismal enough. The gasoline launch had a good start, and they had nothing at hand with which to follow the craft and those on board.

"I'd hate to see the launch wrecked," said Tom. "But I'd like to see those fellows blow themselves up!"

"Well, in that case I could almost stand the loss of the boat," answered the young Southerner, with a faint smile.

They sat down and talked the matter over for quarter of an hour, Fred and Songbird in the meantime bathing their wrists and having them bound up with handkerchiefs. Not only was the launch gone, but their food also.

"I saw a few things left on the Dora," said Dick; "canned stuff and like that, which they forgot to take or ruin. That will give us something to eat."

"We might find a trail out of the swamp to some plantation," suggested Harold Bird, "but that would take time, and I think we ought to be following the launch."

"How?" asked Fred.

"Ve can't schwim," put in Hans.

"Go back for the houseboat and follow them in that. It will be slow, but it will likewise be sure."

"We'll do it," answered Dick.

This time all set out for the houseboat. They followed the first trail that had been taken and, remembering the bad spots, covered the distance without serious mishap. By this time all were hungry, and while Hans and Fred set to work to make a fire in the cook stove and prepare the best meal possible under the circumstances, the others turned the houseboat down the inlet and out into the small lake. It was hard work poling the big craft along, but once in the little lake they were delighted to find that the current was fairly strong towards the big lake and the Mississippi. They used both poles and sweeps and worked like Trojans.

"Dinner is ready!" called Fred at last, and one after another took a seat and ate the canned corn, tomatoes, and salmon which had been made ready. They also had a few crackers and a pot of rather weak coffee, but they were sincerely thankful that matters were not worse.

"The worst of it is, we are not the only sufferers," said Dick to Harold Bird. "The ladies and the girls who have been traveling with us have lost all their valuables—that is, such things as happened to be left on the Dora. Just what is missing they will have to tell us."

"Well, as I said before, I shall do all in my power to bring them to justice. I should think you'd be more than anxious to have this Dan Baxter locked up."

"Yes."

"You say he has been your enemy for years?"

"Yes. When my brothers and I started to go to a boarding school called Putnam Hall, in New York State, we ran across this Baxter. He was annoying Miss Stanhope and her two cousins, Grace and Nellie. We had a row then and there, and ever since that time he has been our bitter enemy and has tried, in a thousand ways, to make trouble for us. Not only that, but his father was a bitter enemy of my father and was locked up. But strange to say, Arnold Baxter has reformed, while Dan seems to go from bad to worse."

"Then you don't think Dan will reform?"

"Hardly. If he does, it will be the surprise of my life," answered the eldest Rover.

The meal, slim as it was, put all on board the houseboat in better humor, and as he washed the dishes Hans hummed a little German ditty to himself. Soon the small lake was left behind, and they found themselves skirting the upper shore of Lake Sico. Nothing was in sight on the broad bosom of this body of water.

"Can the launch be in hiding in some cove?" asked Sam. "We don't want any more tricks played on us."

"It is possible," answered Harold Bird. "Still I think our wisest course will be to get to the river as soon as possible. If the launch has passed out we may find somebody who has seen her."

All worked with vigor, and by nightfall they gained the bayou leading to the mighty river beyond. As they came out they saw a lumber barge tied up not far away.

"Ahoy there!" shouted Dick, using his hands for a speaking trumpet.

"Ahoy!" came the answering shout, from a man on the barge.

"Have you seen anything of a gasoline launch around here?"

"Yes."

"When?"

"About an hour ago."

"Coming from the bayou?"

"Yes."

"Which way did she head?"

"Down the river."

"Are you sure of that, Dillard?" called out Harold Bird.

"Hullo, Mr. Bird, that you?"

"I say, are you sure the launch went down the river?"

"Positive, sir—we watched her out of sight. Was she your boat?"

"She was."

"Stolen?"

"Yes."

"You don't say so! Hope you get her back."

"Who was on board?"

"Four men, so far as we could see. We weren't very close to her."

"We are on the right trail!" cried Tom. "Now the question is, How can we follow her down the river?"

"On the houseboat, of course," answered his elder brother. "If we stop to do anything else we'll lose too much time."

"But that launch can run away from us."

"Perhaps, but you must remember that they'll have to be cautious, because the craft is strange to them. They won't dare to run full speed for fear of blowing up or of striking a snag."

"I vish da struck a hundred of dem snags alretty!" cried Hans.

"Then again, they may tie up as soon as they think they can leave the river with safety. I think we can follow in the houseboat as well as in anything."

"Yes, let us stick to the houseboat," came from the young Southerner. "But wait, pole her over to the barge. Perhaps we can buy some food."

"Yes, let us get food by all means," added Sam.

They were soon beside the lumber barge, which had a comfortable cabin and sleeping quarters. As Harold Bird knew the owner well, there was little difficulty in obtaining provisions and at a reasonable price. Then off those on the Dora pushed, and soon the current of the broad Mississippi carried them out of sight down the stream.

"We must keep a good lookout," said Dick, as night came on. "We don't want to miss them in the dark."

"And we don't want to run into anything either," added Sam.

"Dis ain't kvite der life on der oceans vaves vot I like," observed Hans. "I dink me after all a sail ship oder a steamer been besser, hey?"

"Yes, a sailboat or a steamer would be better just now," answered

Tom. "But we have got to put up with what we happen to have, as the dog said who got lockjaw from swallowing a bunch of keys."

"Did dot dog git dot lockjaw from dem keys?" asked Hans, innocently.

"Sure he did, Hans. You see, they didn't fit the lock to his stomach, so he couldn't digest them."

"Poor dog, vot vos his name?"

"Why, his name was—er—Picker,—but he couldn't pick the lock, so he died."

"Is he teat yet?"

"Is he dead—Say, Hans, what do you mean?"

"Oh, it ton't madder," answered the German boy, and walked away, leaving Tom wondering if the joke had been turned on him or not.

On and on swept the houseboat over the broad bosom of the Mississippi. Fortunately for our friends, it proved a clear night, with countless stars bespangling the heavens.—They had managed to find two lanterns fit for use and each was lit and placed in position. Most of the boys remained on the forward deck, watching anxiously. Dick was at the rudder, steering as Harold Bird directed.

It was not long before something dark loomed up along shore and they knew they had struck one of the numerous levees, or artificial banks, along the Mississippi, put there to prevent the country from being inundated during the freshets. The levee was very high and looked strong enough to withstand almost any pressure that could be brought to bear against it.

"And yet they sometimes give way and cause a terrible amount of drainage," said Harold Bird, in reply to Sam's question. "I have seen the river spread out for miles, and houses and barns carried off to nobody knew where over night."

"Well, I don't think the launch would tie up at the levee, do you?"

"It is not likely. I have an idea those fellows will try to get down to New Orleans."

After that an hour passed without anything unusual happening.

Twice they passed river steamboats, one of them sweeping quite close to the houseboat.

"Why don't you put out more lights—want to be run down?" came the cry.

"Haven't any more lights," answered Tom, and then the two boats swept apart, so no more could be said.

A mile more was passed when Fred set up a cry:

"I see a light ahead, flashing from side to side," he said, and pointed it out.

"It is the acetylene gas lamp," ejaculated Harold Bird, "and it must be aboard of the launch!"

CHAPTER XI

WHAT THE ROCKETS REVEALED

All of those on board of the houseboat watched the flashing light with keen interest. That it came from the gasoline launch none of them doubted.

"If we can only catch up to them," said Tom. "And do it on the sly!"

"We want to be on guard—they may be ready to do some shooting," returned Sam.

"Does you dink da vill shoot?" inquired Hans, anxiously.

"I don't think they will kill more than three or four of us," answered Tom, by way of a joke.

"Vat?" screamed Hans. "Not me, by chiminatics! I ton't vos vant to been shot dree oder seven dimes alretty!"

"I doubt if they'll do any shooting," answered Harold Bird.

"I can't believe that," said Dick, with a shake of his head. "That Sack Todd is a bad one, and Baxter can be very wicked at times. We certainly want to be on guard against any underhanded work."

The launch had been running somewhat across the river, but was now headed straight down the Mississippi.

"We don't seem to be gaining," said Fred, after a silence of several minutes. "It appears to be just as far ahead as when we first saw it."

"We are certainly not gaining much," answered the young Southerner. "But I think we are gaining a little."

Harold Bird was right, they were gaining probably one rod in twenty. Thus, in a little over half an hour, they saw that the launch was almost within hailing distance. The acetylene gas light was thrown ahead and to the right and left, and lit up the surface of the river for a considerable distance. Against the rays of the lamp they could make out four persons in the launch.

"They must be the four we are after," said Dick. "I wish they would turn into shore, at some town. Then we'd have an easier time of it, rounding them up."

"I have an idea!" cried Sam. "Why not follow them until they do land somewhere and go to sleep? We'll have a better chance to capture all of them than in a fight out here. Here, if we get into a row, somebody may fall overboard and be drowned."

"Yes, let us follow them until they stop somewhere," came from Songbird, who had no desire to fight out there on the bosom of the swiftly-flowing Mississippi.

This decided on, they did not attempt to catch up to the launch, but, getting near enough to keep the craft in plain view, held back just a trifle.

"Do you suppose they see us?" asked Fred.

"They may see the houseboat, but they don't know what craft it is, or who is on board," answered Dick.

Presently the launch stopped running and merely drifted with the current. Those in the houseboat saw the gas lamp turned toward the shore.

"I think they are making preparations to land," said Harold Bird.

A moment later the acetylene lamp was turned back and the sharp rays fell full upon the Dora and those on the forward deck.

"Hi! There is the houseboat!" cried Dan Baxter, who was following the rays of light with his eyes.

"That's so!" returned Gasper Pold. "They must be following us!"

"How did they do it so quickly?" questioned Solly Jackson.

"That's a puzzle, but it certainly is the houseboat, and there are three or four of the crowd on board," said Sack Todd.

Those on the launch were amazed to think they had been followed so quickly and for the moment knew not what to do. Then Sack Todd drew his pistol.

"Hi, there!" he yelled. "Keep your distance, if you know when you are well off!"

"They know us right enough," murmured Tom. "And they mean to fight!"

"Go ahead,—we can't afford to land around here!" said Gasper Pold, to Baxter, who had been running the motor of the launch. And soon the power was turned on and the launch started down the river faster than ever.

"They are running away from us!" ejaculated Dick. "Oh, what luck!"

"Stop!" yelled Sam. "Stop, or we'll fire at you!"

"That's the talk," said Harold Bird.

"If you do any firing, so will we!" came back from one of the persons on the Venus.

Then of a sudden the acetylene gas lamp was either turned off or its rays were hidden, for the launch was almost lost in the darkness of the night.

"They were trying to hide," said Fred. "And it looks as if they would succeed," he added, as the launch seemed to fade utterly from view.

"If we only had that gas lamp,—to keep them in view!" sighed Sam.

"Are you certain there is nothing of the kind on board?" questioned Songbird. "Didn't you buy some rockets when we stopped at—"

"Sure I did!" shouted Dick. "Just the thing—if they are still on board. And they may be—for I put them in a closet we don't often use."

Dick started on a hunt and soon put in an appearance with several rockets, such as are generally used on a ship as a signal of distress.

"They'll be good in more ways than one," said Tom. "They will keep those rascals in sight and also let folks know that we need help."

"Py golly! Ve vill haf a regular Fourth of Chuly, hey?" came from Hans.

A rocket was placed in position at the bow end of the houseboat and the eldest Rover touched it off. It sizzed for an instant and then shot forward over the water in the direction of the gasoline launch, making the scene light for the time being. It came down just over the Venus' bow.

"Hi! stop that, or we'll fire at you!" came from the launch, and then a pistol rang out and the ball whistled over the deck of the Dora.

"Are they really shooting at us?" asked Songbird, nervously, while Hans sought the shelter of the cabin in a hurry.

"I reckon not," answered Harold Bird. "That was simply meant as a warning."

Those on the houseboat waited for several minutes and then, imagining the launch was turning to the shore, Dick prepared another rocket.

"Get behind the woodwork," he said. "They may take it into their heads to aim at us when this goes up."

All sheltered themselves and with a rush the second rocket flew skyward. It had not been aimed at the launch, yet it cut the water within a yard of the Venus' side, much to the alarm of those on board.

"They are trying to shoot us with rockets!" yelled Dan Baxter.

"Take that!" said Sack Todd, and fired point-blank at the houseboat. The bullet hit a pane of glass in the cabin window, and there was a jingle followed by a yell from Hans.

"Sthop dot! Ton't kill me! I ain't vos tone noddings alretty! Of you schoot me again I vos haf you but in prison for a hundred years, ain't it!"

"Are you hit, Hans?" questioned Dick, running to the German boy.

"Putty near, Dick. Dot pullet knocked owit der glass chust ven I vos going to look owit!"

"They have hit on something!" came from Harold Bird, who had remained outside, behind a barrel.

"Hit?" queried Sam.

"Yes, they are stuck fast, and we are drifting right on top of them!"

The news proved true, the launch had gotten caught on a sunken tree trunk and was helpless on the bosom of the river, the propeller whirling madly. The houseboat was less than two hundred feet away and coming forward as swiftly as the current could carry her.

"Look out! Don't smash us—we are stuck!" yelled Dan Baxter.

"Sheer off!" came from Solly Jackson. "Sheer off, or we'll all be wrecked!"

It was a position of unexpected and extreme peril, and those on the houseboat realized it as well as those on the launch. Yet what to do our friends did not exactly know.

"Out with the sweeps—on this side!" called out Dick, and ran for the biggest sweep he could find. "Jam over the rudder!" he called to Songbird, who was at the tiller.

The rudder went over in a jiffy and out went three long sweeps. This served to swing the houseboat over several points, but not enough to take her entirely out of the course of the launch.

"We are going to hit as sure as fate!" cried Sam.

"Yes, and we may all go to the bottom," answered Fred.

CHAPTER XII

STUCK ON A SNAG

It was certainly a moment of intense anxiety, both for those on the launch and on the houseboat, and for the time being the fight between the two factions came to an end. A smash-up out there in that swiftly-flowing current might make it necessary for everybody to swim for his life.

"Can't you back the boat?" asked Sack Todd of Dan Baxter. "We must get out somehow!"

Dan Baxter worked over the motor for a few seconds, and just as the houseboat swung closer started the launch backwards. All expected a crash, but it did not come.

"The Dora is stuck!" called out Dick. "We have hit something under water!"

The eldest Rover was right, and slowly the houseboat began to swing around. In the meantime the launch backed away, made a half-circle, and began to move again down the Mississippi.

"They are loose!" called out Sam.

"Yes, and we are fast," answered Harold Bird. "But I am rather glad we didn't run into the launch and smash her completely."

The moving of the launch had caused the sunken tree trunk to turn partly over, and in this position two immense limbs caught the Dora tightly so that, although the houseboat swung broadside to the current, she could get no further.

"They are getting away from us!" cried Tom, as the Venus disappeared from view.

"Don't you dare to follow us any further," called out a voice from the darkness. "If you do, it will be at your peril!"

"It doesn't look as if we were going to follow them right away." grumbled Tom.

"Vos dose rascallions gone alretty?" questioned Hans, coming cautiously from the cabin.

"Yes."

"Dot's goot!"

The lanterns were lowered over the side of the houseboat, and after several minutes of inspection our friends located the source of the trouble.

"If we had the power to back away from that tree we'd be all right," observed Dick. "But as we haven't such power I do not know what we are going to do."

"Maybe we'll have to wait until morning," said Tom. "Then some passing boat can pull us away."

"And in the meantime those rascals will have a good chance to outwit us," said Sam, bitterly. "It's a shame!"

"Let us try to get the sweeps between the tree limbs and the house-boat," suggested Harold Bird. "Perhaps we can thus pry ourselves loose."

All were willing to try the plan, and while the young Southerner took one sweep Dick took another, with Sam and Tom to help them.

It was no easy matter to get the sweeps into position, for there was danger of one or another slipping overboard. To protect themselves each of the workers wound a rope around his waist and made the end fast to a stanchion.

"Now then, all together!" cried Dick, when the sweeps were finally in proper position, and they strained with all their might. Then came a crack, as one sweep broke, and Harold Bird and Sam were hurled flat on their backs on the deck.

"Never mind, better luck next time," said Songbird, as he brought another sweep forward.

They adjusted the new sweep with care and pulled on it gradually.

At first the houseboat refused to budge, but presently it swung around a little and then more and more.

"Hurrah! we are getting her!" yelled Tom. "Now then, all together, as the tomcat said to the boy's with the brickbats."

They strained and the houseboat came loose, but alas! at that moment both sweeps slipped and slowly but surely the Dora swung into her former position and became jammed tighter than before.

"Another failure," sighed Dick.

"I'm about out of breath," said Sam, with a gasp.

"Let me try it," said Fred, and he, Hans, and Songbird set to work, with the others helping. But it was of no avail, the houseboat could not be moved sufficiently to clear herself of the sunken tree trunk with its immense limbs.

"Well, there is one thing to be thankful for," said Dick, as they rested from their labors. "That trunk might have gone through our sides or bottom and sunk us."

During the next hour two steamboats passed them, but not near enough to be asked for help. They cleaned their lanterns and hung them high up, so as to avoid a collision.

"It's queer that no craft came out to learn why the rockets were sent up," said Dick.

"Perhaps they thought some celebration was going on," answered Harold Bird.

"It's nearly two o'clock and I am dead tired," announced Tom. "Any objections to my going to sleep?"

"Not if you can get to sleep," answered his older brother.

"Half of us might as well turn in, while the other half remain on guard," said Sam, and so it was arranged. Two hours later the guard was changed, so that all got some much-needed rest, although a sound sleep was out of the question.

With the coming of morning the youths looked around eagerly for some craft to give them assistance. Yet it was a good hour before a steamboat came down the river and stopped at their call.

"What's wanted?"

"We want to be towed down the river," said Dick. "We'll pay you for the job."

"Are you stuck?"

"Yes, but you can easily pull us back and out."

"Where do you want to go?"

Those on the houseboat had already talked the matter over and decided to move on at least as far as Baraville, about twenty miles from New Orleans. Dick had once heard Sack Todd speak of the place and knew the man was acquainted there, and had also heard Solly Jackson say he had once lived in that locality.

"I'll tow you to Baraville if you wish it," said the captain of the small steamboat. "It will cost you ten dollars."

"All right, but get there as fast as you can," answered Dick. "We are in a big hurry."

A line was thrown out and made fast, and in a few minutes the houseboat was freed from the sunken tree. Then steamboat and houseboat swung around and the journey to Baraville was begun. It did not take long, and by half-past ten o'clock the Dora was tied up at the town levee, much to the astonishment of many colored folks who had never seen such a craft.

The Rovers' first movement was to ask if the launch had stopped there, and from a colored riverman they learned that the Venus had come in very early in the morning and had left again after those on board had gotten breakfast and a box of things—what the negro did not know.

"I heah dem folks talk erbout New Orleans," said the colored man. "I dun 'spect da gone dat way fo' certainly, I do!"

"Did you see the launch leave?" asked Sam.

"I suah did—an' a mighty po'erful smell dat boat did leab behind it!"

"That was the gasoline," said Fred, laughing.

"I 'spect it was, yes, sah," answered the colored man.

"If they went to New Orleans then we ought to go too—and be quick about it," said Dick.

"Don't you want to send some word to the ladies and the girls first?" asked Harold Bird.

"To be sure. We can send a telegram for all, and then send letters, too."

This was done, and the ladies and girls were told not to be alarmed—that all were satisfied everything would come out right in the end.

"No use of worrying them," said Tom. "They can worry after all the trouble is over," and at this quaint remark the others had to smile.

How to get down the river was at first a problem, but it was soon settled by Dick and Harold Bird. It was decided to leave the houseboat in the care of a trustworthy person at Baraville and then charter the small steamboat for the trip to New Orleans. As the captain wanted to go down the river anyway he made the charge for the charter very small, and before noon the craft was on her journey.

Fortunately for our friends the weather remained fine, and had they not been worried over the outcome of what was before them, they would have enjoyed the brief trip on the small steamboat very much. The captain had heard of the capture of the counterfeiters and was surprised to learn that the Rover boys had been the ones to aid in the round-up.

"You've got courage," said he. "I admire what you did. But if I were you I'd fight shy of that Sack Todd. He'll certainly have it in for you, for having broken up that gang."

"I only want to lay my hands on him, that's all," answered Dick. "I am not afraid of him."

"And that Gasper Pold is a bad one too," went on the captain. "I heard about him down in New Orleans. He cheated a lot of people with lottery tickets and policy-playing once, and they got after him hot-footed, and he had to clear out and lay low for awhile."

"Well, in one way the folks who are foolish enough to invest in lottery tickets or play policy deserve to lose their money," put in Sam.

"You are right, lad,—gambling is nothing short of a curse and nobody ought to stand for it. Why, on this very river men have been ruined by gambling, and some have committed suicide and others have become murderers, all because of cards—and drink. One is as bad as the other, and both as bad as can be."

"Of course they don't gamble as they used to," came from Harold Bird. "The times have changed a great deal for the better."

CHAPTER XIII

THE CAPTURE OF SOLLY JACKSON

The Rover boys and their friends from Putnam Hall had never been as far south as New Orleans before, and they viewed the city and its approaches with deep interest. The levees were piled high with cotton, molasses, and other commodities, and more activity was shown than they had witnessed since leaving the Ohio.

The small steamboat had a regular landing-place, but under orders from Dick and Harold Bird the captain took her up and down the levees and also to the other side of the stream. All on board kept their eyes open for a possible view of the launch, but nothing was seen of the Venus.

"It is possible that she has gone further," said Tom. "Wonder if we can't find out from some of the rivermen?"

"We can try anyway," returned Sam. "It doesn't cost money to ask questions."

They spent the remainder of that day in hunting for some trace of the launch and then put up at one of the leading hotels over Sunday. They rested soundly and after dinner felt, as Tom put it, "a hundred per cent. better and some extra." Then they took another walk and made more inquiries.

The captain of the small steamboat had no charter for the next few days, so he was anxious to remain in their employ, and he took them along the waterfront again early Monday morning. During this trip they fell in with another captain who told them he had seen the Venus on Sunday afternoon, with four men on board, puffing down the river.

"I was interested in the launch, so I noticed her particularly," said he. "Two of the men had quite some liquor aboard and I was thinking they might fall overboard, but they didn't." Then he described how the party was dressed, and our friends came to the conclusion that they must be Pold, Todd, Jackson, and Baxter.

"Where could they be going to next?" asked Fred.

"That remains for us to find out—if we can," answered Dick. "All I can think of to do, is to follow them."

"Can't we telegraph ahead to stop the launch and arrest those on board?" questioned Songbird.

"Yes, we can do that."

The authorities were consulted and the telegrams sent. Then off our friends hurried, and were soon on the way down the Mississippi once more.

About ten miles below New Orleans is the entrance to Lake Borge Canal, an artificial waterway connecting the Mississippi with Lake Borge, which opens, through Mississippi Sound, into the Gulf of Mexico. The captain of the small steamboat had an idea the men who had stolen the launch were making for this canal, and he was not mistaken. Arriving at the canal entrance, our friends learned that the launch had been taken through very early in the morning.

"Well, this ends the search so far as I am concerned," said the steamboat captain. "I suppose you want to go on somehow."

"Can't we send word to the other end of the canal?" asked Sam.

"Yes, we can telephone to the station there," answered Harold Bird, and this was done without delay.

"Want the launch Venus, do you?" came back over the wire. "She went through some hours ago.

"Where did she go to?"

"Somewhere on the lake."

This was all the satisfaction they could get, and bidding the steamboat captain goodbye after paying him off, the Rovers and their friends looked around for some means of getting to Lake Borge, a distance of seven or eight miles.

A barge was going through, and they were soon on board. They urged the owner to hurry and offered him big pay, and as a consequence before noon they reached the lake. Here they ran into an old fisherman, who told them that the persons in the launch had had a quarrel with two officers of the law and had sailed off in the direction of Bay St. Louis.

"This is certainly getting to be a long chase," remarked Tom. "First thing we know we'll be following them all the way across the Gulf of Mexico."

"Well, I am willing," answered Dick, promptly.

"And so am I," added Harold Bird. "I intend to bring them to justice if I possibly can."

Again there was a consultation, and the old fisherman told them how they might reach Bay St. Louis, a town of considerable importance on Mississippi Sound. The trip took some time, and on the way they looked around eagerly for some sight of the launch, but the craft did not appear.

At Bay St. Louis came a surprise. The launch had entered the harbor on fire and those on board had had to swim for their lives. The craft had been running at full speed, had struck a mud scow and gone under, and was now resting in eight feet of water and mud.

"Was she burnt very much?" asked Harold Bird, of the person who gave this information.

"I don't think she was," was the answer. "She went down before the flames got very far."

"And what of the rascals who ran, or rather swam, away?" asked Dick.

"They came ashore, went to a hotel, where they dried their clothing and got something to eat, and then went off to get the launch raised."

"I don't believe they intended to raise the launch," said Sam, promptly. "That was only a bluff."

"Exactly what I think," put in Tom. "Those fellows know they'll be followed sooner or later, and they'll try to make themselves scarce."

What to do next our friends scarcely knew. They went to several points along the sound front, but could gain no information of value.

"We've lost them," said Songbird, dismally. "All our long chase for nothing."

They were moving from one dock to another when they saw a man sitting on some bales of cotton, sleeping soundly and snoring lustily.

"Why, isn't that the carpenter who was going to repair the Dora?" cried Sam.

"Sure it is!" answered Tom. "Here is luck!"

"I wonder if those other rascals are near?" questioned Fred.

They looked all around, but soon reached the conclusion that Solly Jackson was alone. Then they shook the fellow and roused him. He had evidently been drinking, but he was now almost sober.

"What's the matter?" he demanded, sleepily. "Lemme alone, Pold."

"Wake up, you rascal!" cried Dick. "You're not on the launch."

"What's the reason I ain't?" stammered Solly Jackson. "Oh, she got on fire, didn't she? Well, let her burn!" And he attempted to go to sleep again.

"You'll wake up!" cried Harold Bird, and between them he and Dick shook the fellow until he was thoroughly aroused. When he realized his position he was greatly alarmed.

"Oh, gentlemen, it's all a mistake," he whined. "I—er—I didn't run off with the launch, or the houseboat either. All a mistake, I tell you!"

"It was a mistake," answered Dick, grimly. "And you'll find it so when you are behind the prison bars."

"Whe—where are the others?"

"That is what we want to know," said Tom. "Where did you leave them?"

"Ain't they here?"

"No. Where were you with them last?"

Solly Jackson scratched his head thoughtfully.

"At the tavern. I had several drinks, and that's the last I knew."

"Did they bring you here and leave you?" asked Sam.

"I reckon they did—I don't know exactly. But, gentlemen, I didn't steal the boats and things, really I didn't. It was Gasper Pold did the trick."

"You aided him," said Tom.

"He said at first he had bought the houseboat and was going to take her to New Orleans. He wanted me to go along and finish the repairs, and I didn't find out what was really up till we got to the Lake Sico bayou. Then he told me that if I didn't stick to him he'd shoot me."

"When did Sack Todd and Dan Baxter join you?" asked Sam.

"Just before we left. I don't know where they came from, but Pold knew Sack Todd well and Todd brought in the young fellow. Then they hid the houseboat in the bushes and stole what they could, and afterwards ran off with the launch."

"Yes, but you helped the others to make us prisoners," came from Songbird, severely.

"I did it because I had to—Pold said he'd shoot me if I went back on him. Mr. Bird,"—Solly Jackson turned to the young Southerner, —"you know I ain't no bad man like Pold an' that sort."

"I know you are weak-minded and weak-kneed," answered Harold Bird, in disgust. "But you stood in with those rascals and you must take the consequences."

"It's mighty hard on a fellow as ain't done nothin'!"

"Where did the other fellows go?" demanded Tom.

"I don't know—reckon they left me when I went to sleep here."

"Didn't they mention any place?" demanded Dick, sternly. "Come, if you expect us to be easy on you, you must tell us all you know."

"They did," answered Solly Jackson, after scratching his head again. "Gasper Pold said he thought of going to Tampa, Florida, where he has several friends. That young Baxter said he'd like to go to Tampa, and Sack Todd said he might go along. Then they talked of going over to Mobile, to get a steamer there for Tampa, but Pold said it wouldn't do, as all the steamboat landings and railroad offices might be watched. So then Pold said he would look around and see if he couldn't find some boat that was going to Tampa from here."

"A steamer?" queried Harold Bird.

"Either that or a sailing vessel, he didn't much care which. He said a sailing vessel might be safer, especially if they could ship without those on shore knowing it."

This was practically all that Solly Jackson could tell them. As he grew more sober he seemed truly repentant of his misdeeds. He said Gasper Pold had plied him with liquor before running away with the Dora, and that had he been perfectly sober he should never have aided in such a rascally bit of work. That he had been nothing more than a tool from start to finish there could be little doubt. He agreed to go with them and do all he could to locate his former companions, and also do what he could towards having the gasoline launch raised and put in order.

CHAPTER XIV

ON A GULF STEAMER

"Well, now for a life on the ocean wave!" came from Tom.

"Und a houses on der rollings deeps," put in Hans.

"And may the enemy be captured in short order," came from Harold Bird.

"All well enough to hope that, but I am afraid we have some work before us, perhaps something we won't like," said Dick, seriously. "Those men know that the prison is staring them in the face, and they will do all in their power to escape. If cornered they may put up a stiff fight."

"Well, we can put up a fight too," answered Sam.

The conversation took place on the forward deck of the Mascotte, a gulf steamer running from Mobile to Tampa and other points on the Florida coast. Two days had passed since the boys had arrived at Bay St. Louis and in that time they had accomplished several things of more or less importance.

It had been an easy matter to obtain all possible information from Solly Jackson, and for the time being the fellow was in the hands of the law, awaiting further developments. He had promised, if the others were captured, that he would give evidence against them, and in return for this Dick and Harold Bird said they would be easy on the carpenter when he came up for trial.

The gasoline launch had been raised without much trouble and towed to a shipyard, where she was to undergo repairs. The craft was not damaged a great deal, but would need a new gasoline tank and some new seats. Fortunately the gasoline supply had been low at the time the fire broke out, otherwise those on board would have been blown sky-high.

After numerous inquiries Tom and Sam Rover had learned that Pold, Todd, and Dan Baxter had taken passage for Tampa on a schooner named the Dogstar. The vessel carried a light load of lumber consigned to a firm that was erecting a new winter hotel on Tampa Bay, and expected to make a fairly quick passage across the gulf.

The Rovers and their friends had taken the train from Bay St. Louis to Mobile, after first sending messages to Mrs. Stanhope, Mrs. Laning, and the girls. At Mobile they had just been in time to catch the Mascotte and had been equally fortunate in securing several vacant staterooms.

"We'll head them off this time," said Tom, yet this was by no means certain, it depending somewhat on the quickness of the trip made by the lumber schooner. The Mascotte was by no means a first-class steamer, and it had been a question, the day before the voyage was undertaken, if she had not better be laid up for repairs to her engine and boilers. But of this our friends knew nothing.

As soon as the trip was begun Dick and Harold Bird had an interview with the captain of the steamer and told the latter how anxious they were to get track of the Dogstar. To their dismay, however, the captain proved to be anything but agreeable and said he could not bother himself over their personal affairs, even when offered pay to do so.

"He's a regular lemon," said Tom. "I don't think he'd do a favor for anybody."

"And this steamer is a tub," answered Sam. "I shouldn't wish to travel very far in her."

Yet with it all the boys felt in pretty fair spirits as they gathered on the deck and talked matters over. But in less than an hour they were in open rebellion.

They went to the dining room for dinner and were served with food that was scarcely fit to eat. As they had paid for first-class accommodations all found fault.

"Waiter, bring me some meat that isn't burnt," said Sam.

"And bring me some that is fresh," added Harold Bird.

"And bring me a cup of coffee that is worth more than ten cents a pound," came from Songbird. "This is nothing but mud."

"Even this bread is next door to being sour," said Fred.

"Yah, dis vos der vorst tinner vot I efer see alretty!" was Hans' comment. "I vos make a kick py der cabtain, ain't it!"

"Sorry, gen'men," said the waiter. "But dat meat am de best we have, an' dar ain't no udder kind ob coffee an' bread, sah!"

"Whose fault is it, the cook's or the captain's?" asked Tom.

At this question the waiter shrugged his shoulders. Then he leaned over and whispered into Tom's ear.

"Wish yo' would make a kick—I hates to serve sech food—'deed I does!"

The boys left the table half hungry and so did the other passengers. Dick walked up to one of the others.

"Don't you think we ought to make them serve us with better food?" he asked, flatly.

"I do, sir," was the answer of the passenger. "But the cook said it was the best he had. He said we might go to the captain or to anybody we please. He is going to leave the boat when we arrive at Tampa."

Without more ado Dick, Harold Bird, and about a dozen others sought out Captain Fretwood, who was in his private cabin.

"What is it?" demanded the officer, eying the crowd sourly.

"We have come to complain of the food served at dinner," said Dick. "It was so poor we could not eat it."

"Oh, the food is all right," answered the captain in an overbearing tone.

"No, it is not all right," put in Harold Bird.

"We paid for first-class accommodations and we want first-class food," put in Tom, with spirit.

"That's the talk," came from several in the crowd.

"See here, I am not to be dictated to by a lot of boys!" cried Captain Fretwood, angrily. "We are giving you good food, and that is all there is to it."

"It's a fraud!" cried Sam.

"A downright imposition," added Songbird.

"Our tickets read 'First Cabin with Meals,'" said Fred. "Those meals aren't good enough for steerage passengers. Unless you give us something better—"

"Ha! do you threaten me on my own ship?" bellowed the captain.

"We certainly do!" said Dick, as Fred glanced at him questioningly.

"I can put you in irons for it, young man!"

"No, you can't. We are not going to touch you or any of your crew. But unless you serve us with first-class food from now on I, for one, shall make a complaint against you as soon as we land, and have you arrested."

At this announcement the face of the captain of the Mascotte grew purple with rage. He stepped forward as if to strike Dick. But the latter stood his ground, looked the irate officer full in the eyes, and the man paused.

"We have had trouble enough without your adding to it," said Harold Bird. "We ask only that which is due us."

"The young man is perfectly right," said an elderly passenger. "The food is horrible. If he makes a complaint to the authorities I shall sustain him."

"So will I," added several.

"All right, have your own way," grumbled the captain. "I see you are bound to get me in a hole. If the food wasn't good it was the fault of the cook."

"He says it is your fault, and he is going to leave you at the end of this trip."

"Bah! Well, we'll see. If he can't serve the food properly cooked I'll be glad to get rid of him."

After that an all-around discussion ensued, lasting quarter of an hour. Led by the boys the passengers were very outspoken, and as a

consequence the next meal was fairly good, although not exactly first
-class.

"We tuned him up, that's certain," said Sam.

"I am glad you did," said a passenger sitting opposite. "I was afraid
I should be starved to death before we reached land."

"He'll have it in for us," said Fred. "Every time he looks at me he
glares like a wild beast."

"We'll keep our eyes open," said Dick. "But I don't think he'll do
anything. He knows we were in the right. I reckon he's more of a
talker than anything else," and in this surmise the eldest Rover was
correct.

During the afternoon a heavy mist swept over the gulf and the
speed of the Mascotte had to be slackened. Two men were placed on
watch besides the pilot, but they could see little.

"This is going to delay us still more," said Tom, and he was right.
About six o'clock they came near crashing into another steamboat,
and after that the forward movement was almost checked entirely.

All on board felt it would be a night of more or less peril, and consequently the trouble over the meals was forgotten. The captain
paced the deck nervously, and the pilot and other watchers strained
their eyes to pierce the gloom.

"I must say, I don't feel much like turning in," remarked Sam. "I
can't tell why it is, either."

"I feel myself as if something unusual was in the air," answered
Tom.

"Boys," said Dick to his brothers, "if anything should happen,
stick together."

"To be sure," came from Sam and Tom.

"But do you think something will really happen?" added the
youngest Rover.

"I don't know what to think. I know this steamer is worse than an
old tub, and I know that the mist is getting so thick you can cut it
with a knife."

"I wish we were on shore again, Dick."

"So do I."

"Py chiminatics!" came from Hans. "Owit on der deck you can't see your face before your nose alretty!"

"Of course you know what this means, Hans," answered Tom, who was bound to have a little fun in spite of the seriousness of the situation.

"Vot does dot mean?"

"You know they have great earthquakes down here, and great volcanoes."

"Vell, vot of dot?"

"When it gets so misty as this then look out for a fearful earthquake and a great volcanic eruption."

"You ton't tole me!" gasped the German youth. "Say, I ton't vont no earthkvakes, not much I ton't!"

"Maybe it won't do much harm—only sink the ship," put in Sam, taking his cue from Tom.

"Sink der ship? Den ve peen all drowned, ain't it? Say, Sam, how kvick you dink dem earthkvakes come, hey?"

"Oh, some time to-night," answered the youngest Rover.

"Mine cracious! Ve peen all killed asleep!" groaned Hans. "Say, I dink I ton't go py der ped, not me!" he added, earnestly.

At that moment came a cry from the deck. It was followed by a thump and a crash that threw all of the boys flat on the floor of the cabin of the steamer.

CHAPTER XV

THE CASTAWAYS OF THE GULF

"It vos der earthkvake!" yelled Hans, as he scrambled to his feet. "Der oceans vos all busted up alretty! Safe me!" And he ran for the cabin doorway.

"We must have struck something in the fog!" cried Dick, as he, too, arose. "Oh!"

Another crash had come, heavier than the first, and the Mascotte careened far over to port. Then came wild screams from the deck, followed by orders delivered in rapid succession. All in a moment the passengers were in a panic, asking what had been struck and if the steamer was going down.

The Rovers and their friends tried to make their way on deck, but another shock threw Fred and Songbird back into the cabin and partly stunned them. Then Harold Bird ran to his stateroom, to get a pocketbook containing his money.

Out on the deck all was misty, the lights gleaming faintly through the darkness. To one side loomed up another steamer, of the "tramp" variety, heavily laden with a miscellaneous cargo from Central American ports.

"The Mascotte is going down!" was the cry, as the steamer gave a suspicious lurch. Then came another crash, and before he knew it Dick Rover went spinning over the side, into the dark and misty waters of the gulf!

It was certainly a time of extreme peril, and had not poor Dick kept his wits about him he must surely have been drowned. Down he went over his head and it was fully quarter of a minute before he came to the surface once more, spluttering and clashing the water from his eyes. He looked around, felt something hard hit him, and then went under once more.

He knew he was near the bottom of some ship and held his breath as long as possible. When he again arose it was to gasp for air. Now he was free of the ship, and the rolling waters of the Gulf of Mexico lay all around him.

His first impulse was to cry out for help, and again and again he raised his voice. But the confusion on board the Mascotte and the other steamer was so great that nobody heard him, or, at least, paid any attention.

Dick strained his eyes and could make out the steamer lights dimly. He was about to yell again, when something floated near and struck him down once again. But as he came up he caught at the object and held fast to it. It was a large crate, empty, and with considerable difficulty he climbed on top.

"This is better than nothing," he thought. And then, catching his breath, he set up a long and lusty cry, in the meantime watching with a sinking heart the lights of both steamers as they faded from view.

A quarter of an hour passed—it seemed much longer to poor Dick,—and the lights disappeared entirely. His heart sank like lead in his bosom.

"They won't come back for me now," he reasoned. "Perhaps the steamboat is sinking and the others have enough to do to think of saving themselves."

The crate Dick was upon was not extra large, and it merely allowed him to keep his head and shoulders out of water. Fortunately the night was not cold, so he suffered little from his involuntary bath. But he realized the seriousness of his situation and was correspondingly sober.

"I must be a good way from land," he reasoned. "I'll have my own troubles saving myself, even if the mist clears away."

Another quarter of an hour went by and then Dick thought he heard voices. He strained his ears.

"I think Dick went overboard too, although I am not sure," came, in Sam's tones.

"Yah, I dink dot," answered Hans Mueller. "Und I dink Tom he falls ofer also alretty!"

"Hullo, there!" cried Dick.—"Is that you, Sam?"

"Who calls?" came the answering query. "It is I, Dick Rover!"

"Dick!" came from Sam and Hans.

"Where are you?"

"This way!" called Sam, and kept on calling until Dick drew closer and at last made out his brother and the German boy clinging to another crate.

"This is lucky—as far as it goes," said Sam. "Are you hurt?"

"Not at all. And you?"

"I got a scratch on my wrist, that is all, and Hans says he twisted his left ankle a little. But we are glad we weren't drowned."

"What of the others?"

"I am almost sure Tom went overboard. I think the others remained on the steamer."

"Was she sinking?"

"I think she was. I heard somebody say there was a big hole stove in her near the port bow."

After that the three youths pulled the two crates together. A grass rope was fastened to one of the affairs and they used this in joining the two, and then the castaways made themselves as comfortable as possible on their improvised raft.

The thought that Tom might have been drowned cast a gloom over Sam and Dick and also made Hans feel bad. Consequently but little was said for the next few hours. All kept their eyes strained for the sight of some friendly light, but none came to view.

"How many miles do you think we are from shore?" asked Sam, presently.

"I haven't any idea," answered Dick. "At least fifty or a hundred."

"Ve vill nefer see der land again!" groaned Hans. "I vish ve had gone to dot Dampa py railroad drain, ain't it!"

"Well, even railroad trains occasionally have smash-ups," answered Dick, philosophically.

At last it began to grow light and with the coming of morning the mist lifted a trifle, so that they were able to see around them. A gentle breeze was blowing, causing the bosom of the gulf to ruffle up. Sam climbed up to the top of the crates.

"See anything?" queried his brother.

"Well, I never!" ejaculated the youngest Rover. "If that doesn't beat the nation!"

He pointed off to their left and then all looked—and actually laughed. And well might they do so.

There, on the waters, rode a rude raft made of several empty boxes and crates. On the top of this affair stood a campstool, and on the stool sat Tom Rover, making himself as comfortable as possible.

"Tom!" the others yelled in concert, and the fun-loving Rover looked around eagerly.

"Hello, you!" he called back. "How many?"

"Three," answered Sam. "Dick, Hans, and myself."

"Good enough."

"You certainly seem to be taking it easy," said Dick, as the two rude rafts floated close to each other.

"Well, why not take it easy if it doesn't cost any more?" demanded Tom, coolly. "I either had to sit on the chair or in the water, and I preferred to sit on the chair."

"Do you know anything about the others, Tom?"

"No, but I am afraid they are drowned," and now the fun-loving Rover became serious. "What makes you think that?" asked Sam.

"I think the steamer went down with nearly everybody on board."

"Dot is terrible!" burst out Hans. "Poor Fred! Und poor Songpird! Vot vill der folks say ven da hear dot?" And he shook his head, dubiously.

"And poor Harold Bird!" added Dick. He had taken a strong liking to the young Southerner.

As it grew lighter those on the bosom of the gulf looked vainly for some sign of land or a sail, but hour after hour passed and nothing came to view but the waters under them and the mist and sky overhead.

"I am more than hungry," grumbled Tom. "I didn't get half

enough to eat on that steamer and now I could lay into almost anything."

"Ditto here," answered his younger brother.

"Der poat must haf gone town," said Hans. "Of not, den da vould look aroundt and pick us ub, hey?"

"I don't believe Captain Fretwood would put himself out to look for us," answered Dick. "He hated our whole crowd and would gladly get rid of us."

A little later Sam shifted his position and chanced to place a hand in one of his coat pockets.

"Here's luck!" he cried. "Not much, but something." And he drew forth a thick cake of sweet chocolate, done up in tinfoil and paper.

"Oh, it's salted and will make us thirsty," said Dick.

The chocolate was examined and found to be in fairly good condition, and despite the salt they could not resist the temptation to divide the cake and eat it up. As my readers must know, chocolate is very nourishing and they felt much better after the brief lunch, although very thirsty.

"I bought that on the train from Bay St. Louis to Mobile," explained the youngest Rover. "Sorry now I didn't get half a dozen."

"And a bottle of lemon soda with it," added Tom, who was bound to have a little fun no matter how serious the outlook.

Slowly the morning wore away. About eleven o'clock it looked as if the sun might come out, but soon it clouded over as before and then the mist began to crawl up.

"This is terrible," sighed Sam, at last. "Dick, what can we do?"

"I don't know, Sam. If we knew in what direction the land lay we might make some effort to reach it."

"We couldn't paddle the rafts fifty or a hundred miles."

"I am in hope that some steamer or sailing vessel will come this way and pick us up," answered Dick.

Then a silence fell on the little crowd. Matters were growing serious indeed, and all wondered how the adventure would end.

CHAPTER XVI

A DESERTED STEAM YACHT

"Dick, am I mistaken, or do I see a vessel over yonder?"

Tom asked the question, as he suddenly straightened up and took a long look over to where the mist had temporarily lifted.

"It certainly does look like a ship of some sort," answered Dick, gazing forward with equal eagerness.

"Shall ve call owid?" asked Hans.

"It is too far off."

"Is she coming this way?" asked Sam, who had gotten so much salt water in his eyes that he could not see very well.

"I am not sure if it is a ship," said Tom. "But it is certainly something."

"Let us try to paddle closer," suggested his older brother, and all set to work; Tom using the folded campstool, and the others some bits of boards from the crates.

Very slowly they approached the object, until they felt certain it was a vessel, a steam yacht, as they made out a few minutes later. But no smoke curled from the funnel of the craft, nor could they make out anybody on the deck.

"Yacht ahoy!" yelled Dick, when he felt that his voice might be heard.

To this hail there was no answer, and although the boys strained their eyes to the utmost, they saw nobody moving on the craft ahead.

"Yacht ahoy!" screamed Tom, using his hands as a trumpet. "Yacht ahoy!"

Still there was no answer, nor did a soul show himself. The curiosity of the castaways was aroused to the highest pitch, and as vigorously as they could they paddled to the side of the steam yacht. The craft was not a large one, but seemed to be of good build and in first-class trim. The wheel was lashed fast, causing her to ride fairly well in the faint breeze. Not a sail was set.

"Ahoy! ahoy!" yelled all of the boys in concert.

"Vos you teat, alretty?" asked Hans. "Of you vos, vy ton't you tole somepoty?"

"Gracious, do you think all on board are dead?" cried Sam.

"Either that or else the owners belong to a deaf and dumb asylum," responded Tom.

The castaways continued to call out and in the meantime brought their rude raft close to the side of the steam yacht. As the vessel slipped past them slowly, they threw a bit of rope to the rudder post and made fast.

"Everybody must be below and asleep," said Dick, "although I never before heard of such strange proceedings."

"Nor I," came from Sam. "But the question is, Are we going on board or not?"

"Are we? Of course we are!" burst out Tom. "They couldn't keep me off with a pitchfork. I want a drink of water if nothing else, and I am bound to have it."

"Aboard the yacht!" yelled Dick again. "Why don't you show yourselves and say something? Are you all deaf?"

Still no answer, and the boys looked at each other in amazement.

"Am I dreaming?" demanded Tom.

"Maybe the ship is a—a—phantom?" whispered Sam, and gave a little shiver.

"Well, I am going on board, even if it's the Flying Dutchman himself," cried Tom, bravely.

"Flying Dutchmans?" queried Hans. "Der vos no Dutchmans vot fly, vos dare?"

"Tom is speaking of a phantom ship with a phantom crew, I guess," said Sam. "Tom, how are you going to get on deck?" he added, to his brother.

This was a question Tom could not answer at once. The rail of the steam yacht was some feet above their heads and how to reach it was a problem.

"You can take the ropes from the rafts," suggested Dick. "Perhaps we won't want them any longer."

They took the ropes, tied them together, and Tom threw one end upward. After several failures he got the rope around the rail and the end down within reach, and then he went up hand over hand, in true sailor fashion, for Tom had been a first-class climber from early childhood, "Always getting into mischief," as his Aunt Martha had been wont to say.

"Don't you fellows want to come up?" asked the fun-loving Rover, as soon as he was safe.

"Certainly we do," answered Dick. "Go on, Hans and Sam. I can wait till last."

It was not so easy for Hans to get up and Tom at the top and Dick at the bottom had to aid him. Then Sam went up like a monkey, and the eldest Rover followed, and the crates and boxes, with the campstool, were allowed to drift away.

Once on board the steam yacht the Rovers and Hans looked around with keen curiosity. Not a soul was on deck, in the upper cabin, or in the tiny wheelhouse.

"This is enough to give a fellow the creeps!" declared Sam. "I must say I almost hate to go below."

"Just the way I feel," added Tom. "Perhaps we've run into some great tragedy."

"Everything on deck is in apple-pie order," was Dick's comment. "It certainly is a mystery. But I am going below."

"Wait, Dick!" cried Sam. "Would it not be as well to arm yourself?"

"Perhaps," was the reply, and then all of the "boys procured belaying pins or whatever was handy, with which to ward off a possible attack.

"Maybe they had a lion on board and he ate the whole crew up," suggested Tom.

"Say, of der vos a lion—" began Hans, drawing back.

"Oh, Tom is fooling," interrupted Dick. "They don't carry a menagerie on a vessel like this. Why, this is a gentleman's pleasure yacht."

"Well then, bring on the gentleman," responded the irrepressible Tom. "I shouldn't like anything better than to be introduced to him."

They had almost passed to the last step of the companionway when Sam called a sudden halt.

"Boys, perhaps, after all, we had better keep out of that cabin," he said.

"Why, Sam?"

"This may be a pest ship. The whole crew may have died of yellow fever, or something like that!"

At this announcement all looked at each other with added alarm showing in their faces. A pest ship! The idea filled them with horror.

"If it's that—and we've caught the fever—" began Tom.

"Oh, I vish I vos home, oder at school!" groaned Hans, beginning to shake from head to foot. "Of ve catch der yellow fefer ve peen all teat in a veek!"

For several seconds there was silence, then Dick walked down the last step of the companionway and threw the door below open with a bang.

"I am going to find out what this means," muttered the eldest Rover. "If we are to catch the fever, maybe we've got it already." And he walked into the cabin, and one after another the others followed.

All was in as good order as on deck. On the table lay several books and magazines, one opened and turned face downward as if just placed there.

"Somebody has been reading," murmured Sam. "What did he stop for?" He picked up the magazine and read the heading of one of the articles, "Famous Suicides of Modern History." "Ugh! what delightful literature to read. Just the thing for the young ladies' department of a public library!"

Dick had moved forward to one of the staterooms. With caution he opened the door and peeped in. The apartment was empty, but the berth looked as if it had recently been used.

"Hullo, somebody has been camping out in here," he called. "The bed is mussed up and here's a suit of clothes hanging on the wall."

"And a pair of slippers on the floor," added Sam, over his shoulder.

Gradually the boys grew bolder, and traveled from one stateroom to another and then to the dining room and the cook's galley. Not a person was to be found anywhere. In the galley some cooking had been done and several pans and pots were dirty, but that was all.

"Water!" cried Tom, coming to a cooler. He got the cup and took a long drink, and the others followed.

"And something to eat," added Sam, with satisfaction. "Owner or no owner, I am going to have a square meal just as soon as this inspection is over."

"I dink I sthart now," commented Hans, reaching for a box of crackers. He helped himself and passed them around, and soon all were munching.

From the cook's galley they visited the engine room. The machinery appeared to be in perfect order, the bunkers were half-full of coal, and the firebox was still somewhat warm. But the place was totally deserted.

"This is a deserted steam yacht," said Dick, at last. "I do not think there is a soul on board. We are in absolute possession."

CHAPTER XVII

IN UNDISPUTED POSSESSION

It was a remarkable state of affairs and it took the Rover boys and the German youth a full hour to comprehend it. During that time they explored the steam yacht from end to end and then sat down to eat such a meal as they could fix up hastily. They had canned meat and vegetables, coffee and biscuits, and some canned fruit.

"Dick, how do you solve this mystery?" asked Tom, while they were eating.

"I can't solve it at all," answered his brother. "It is beyond me."

"By the papers we found downstairs I should say the yacht might belong to a man named Roger Leland," put in Sam. "But that doesn't help us out any, for none of us ever heard of that individual."

"If there had been a storm we might think the persons on board had been swept away," went on Dick. "But we haven't had a heavy storm for some time."

"And the yacht hasn't run into anything, for she isn't damaged in the least."

"If we take her into port we can claim salvage," said Sam.

"Certainly, Sam, and heavy salvage too," came from Tom. "But I must say I'd let a dollar or two of that salvage slip right now just to know the explanation of this mystery. Why, it's like a romance!"

"It's a grand good thing for us," said Dick. "If we hadn't found this steam yacht we might have died of hunger and thirst."

"Yah, dot's so," answered Hans. "Of you blease, Dom, I takes me anudder cub of coffee, hey?"

"Hans, that makes four you've had already!"

"Vell, I vos alful try," answered the German youth, complacently.

"The best of it is, the yacht seems to be fairly well stocked with food and water," was Dick's comment, after a pause. "We'll not starve to death, even if it takes a week to reach port."

"Why, we ought to reach port in a couple of days!" cried Sam. "Some of these steam yachts can run very fast."

"So they can—with a competent engineer. But who is going to be the engineer? and who the pilot?"

"Oh, we can pilot her," declared Tom, loftily. "It's as easy as licking cream, as the cat said."

"Maype you vos run us on der rocks," put in Hans.

"I don't think there are many rocks out here—but we'll have to consult the chart," said Dick. "Oh, I think we can pilot her to some port. But I must confess I don't know much about running an engine."

"We'll make her go somehow," answered Tom. "Even if I have to shove the piston rod myself," and at this remark both of his brothers had to laugh.

The more they thought of it the more wonderful did the situation appear to be. It was so wonderful that for the balance of that day they allowed the craft to drift as before. Tom and Sam started up a fair-sized fire under the boiler, after making certain that the latter was more than half-full of water. They knew enough about an engine to locate the safety valve and saw that this was in working order.

"Now, if we get up steam we won't be blown sky-high anyway," said Sam.

While Sam and Tom were experimenting in the engine room, Dick and Hans tried to make themselves familiar with the wheel and the things on deck, and the oldest Rover studied the chart found in the cabin, and the compass.

"I think we are about here," said Dick, when all came together in the cabin, and he traced a circle on the chart with a lead pencil. "Now if that is so, then we'll have to steer directly southeast to reach Tampa Bay."

"Hurrah for Captain Dick!" cried Tom. "Dick, you get your diploma as soon as we land."

"Well, isn't that right?"

"It certainly is according to the map," answered Sam.

"So all you and Tom have got to do is to furnish the power—and not blow us up—and then you get your diplomas too."

"Vot do I got?" asked Hans.

"Oh, you get a big Limburger cheese," cried Tom.

"Vell, dot's putty goot too," answered the youth of Teutonic extraction.

"We'll arrange it this way," said Dick. "Tom can be engineer, Sam fireman, myself pilot, and Hans can be admiral and crew combined."

"Vot does dot crew to?" asked Hans, eagerly.

"Oh, the crew swabs the deck and keelhauls the anchor," answered Tom. "In between times you thread the yardarm, too."

"Vell, den I vill haf mine hands full, ain't it!"

"You eat so much you ought to do some work," said Sam. "If you don't work you'll get as fat as a barrel."

With the coming of night our young friends looked to the lanterns of the steam yacht and refilled those which were empty at an oil barrel stored in the bow of the craft. Then they lit up, and also lit up the cabin.

"I think we may as well cook ourselves a real dinner for this evening," said Dick. "No makeshift affair either."

All were willing, and an hour and a half later they sat down to the table and ate as good a meal as the stores of the steam yacht afforded. Evidently the craft belonged to some person of good taste, for the eatables were of the very best.

"There, that puts new life into a fellow!" declared Dick, after the repast was over. "If I only knew what had become of the Mascotte and the other fellows—knew that our friends were safe—I'd feel quite happy."

"Oh, don't speak of the Mascotte!" answered Sam, with a shiver. "I can't bear to think that Fred and Songbird have been drowned!"

"Let us hope for the best," said Tom, with a sigh. And for the moment all traces of fun disappeared from his countenance.

Thinking it might be a good plan to cast anchor over night, they attempted to do so. But although they let out all the rope and chain, no bottom could be found.

"The water is certainly deep here," said Dick, after the anchor had been brought up again. "I don't think there is any danger of striking rocks."

"Not unless the steam yacht sinks a mile or two," said Tom, with a grin.

It was decided that one person should remain on watch during the night, to report any vessel that might pass and to watch the fire under the boiler. Dick said he would stay up, and Tom told his brother to call him at two in the morning.

"And call me at four," said Sam. "I want to do my share."

The night proved to be as misty as that previously passed, and although first Dick and then Sam and Tom kept their eyes on the alert, nothing was seen or heard of any other vessel. Once Dick fancied he heard the faraway toot of a foghorn, but the sound, whatever it was, was not repeated.

By morning it was raining. At first only a few drops came down, but then it began to pour, so that all were glad to remain under shelter. Hans and Sam prepared breakfast, while Tom looked after the engine and the fire and Dick kept watch on deck.

"It is going to be a corker," was Dick's comment, when he came in for something to eat. "The rain is so thick now you can't see a dozen yards in any direction."

"Let us hope that the rain will clear away the mist," said Sam. "Then perhaps we'll have some sunshine for a change."

"It's all right, if only it doesn't start to blow," answered Tom. "But you must remember that they have some pretty fierce storms down here."

The rain continued to come down as hard as ever and kept up until near noon. In the meantime, however, Sam and Tom got up enough steam to run the yacht at a low rate of speed.

"We can try her that way first," said Tom. "Then, if it's O. K., we'll give her a hundred pounds or so."

"Now, Tom, be careful of that engine!" pleaded Dick. "It won't do to monkey too much."

"Oh, I'll be careful, Dick. I don't want to be blown up any more than you do."

"Remember the old saying, 'The more haste the less speed,'" warned the big brother.

It was with a peculiar thrill that Dick took his place in the wheelhouse and rang the bell for the engine to start. Tom, below, was equally excited as he turned on the power. There was a peculiar hissing and bubbling, but the propeller did not turn.

"What's the matter?" called down Dick, through the speaking tube. "Didn't you hear my signal?"

He listened for a reply, but instead of Tom's voice he heard the fierce hissing of steam. Then, of a sudden, came a yell from Tom.

"Shut off that steam, Sam! Quick! or I'll be scalded to death!"

CHAPTER XVIII

IN PERIL OF STEAM

As quickly as he could, Dick rushed from the wheelhouse and toward the companionway leading to the engine room.

"Vot's der madder?" bawled Hans, who was at the rail, waiting for the steam yacht to start.

"Tom's in trouble," ejaculated the eldest Rover, and went down the stairs four steps at a time, with the German youth behind him.

The engine room was full of steam, so that for the moment Dick could see little. A pipe running along one side of the engine had burst, and Tom was hemmed in a corner. To get out he would have to pass through the furious outpouring of steam, which might scald him to death.

Not far away was Sam, frantically trying to turn the steam off. But the youngest Rover's knowledge of engines and marine machinery was limited and, while he fussed around, the steam in the narrow engine room kept growing thicker and thicker.

"Get down on the floor, Tom!" yelled Dick, as he took in the situation. "Maybe you can crawl out."

Tom did as urged, and like a snake he attempted to crawl from his position of peril. But when he was only halfway he got stuck.

"I—I can't make it!" he panted, trying to worm along. "I—I'm too big."

"Can you go back—I see a door behind you," said Dick.

Tom went back, and as he did this Dick ran out of the engine room and to one of the coal bunkers. Here was the door the eldest Rover had seen. It was closed and barred and somewhat rusty, and he had to exert all his strength to make it budge.

"Quick! quick!" came faintly from Tom. "I can't stand this much longer!"

"This way out, Tom!" called Dick, as the door at last flew open. In the cloud of steam that rushed into the coal bunker Dick saw his brother faintly, and caught him by the arm and pulled him forward. In a moment more both were safe.

"Sam, are you all right?" yelled Dick, rushing again to the engine-room door proper.

"Whe—where's Tom?"

"Safe."

"Oh! then I'll come out," and Sam staggered into the fresh air.

"Mine cracious! vos der ship going to plow up!" gasped Hans, who had stood looking on with his hair standing on end.

"I don't think so," answered Dick. "The steam will soon blow itself away. You didn't have very much pressure; did you, Tom?"

"No, but it was too much when the pipe burst. Gosh! I was afraid I was going to be boiled alive!" and he shuddered.

"It's about gone now," came from Sam, who was watching at the doorway. "It isn't hissing nearly as much as it did." He was right, and presently the hissing ceased entirely. Then Sam, Dick, and Hans opened all the portholes and doors, to let out the steam, and soon the scare was over. But Tom felt "shaky in the legs," as he termed it, for some hours afterwards.

"I suppose I should have tested all those pipes and valves as soon as I had just a little steam," said the fun-loving Rover. "There is where I wasn't a good engineer. Well, one thing is certain, nothing gave way but the single pipe."

"And that could happen on any steamer," answered Dick. "Any engine is liable to a breakdown of this kind. The question is, Are we machinists enough to repair the break? If we are not, then we'll have to let the steam power go and hoist some sails."

"Oh, that would be slow work!" cried Sam. "Let us try to fix the pipe. I saw some extra pieces in the tool room. Maybe one of them will fit."

DICK SAW HIS BROTHER FAINTLY, AND CAUGHT HIM BY THE
ARM AND PULLED HIM FORWARD.

With the engine room cleared of steam they inspected the split pipe. It was a piece exactly two feet long, and they looked over the pieces in the tool room and found one just half an inch shorter.

"I think that will do," said Dick. "We won't be able to couple it on quite so tightly as the other was but we can pack it well, and I guess it will last till we reach some port."

The tool room was supplied with the necessary wrenches and all of the boys spent two hours in fitting in the new piece of pipe. Then they inspected the other pipes and the engine, but everything appeared to be in first-class shape.

The fire had been allowed to die down while the repairs were going on, and was not started up again until the work had been completed.

"Say, don't I look like a nigger?" demanded Tom, as he put down some tools. "If I don't, I feel black from head to foot."

"You are certainly pretty grimy," answered Sam, with a laugh. "But I am that myself."

"We'll all have to go in for a good wash," said Dick.

"Vy ton't you chump oferpoard?" demanded Hans, who was pretty dirty himself.

"Say! just the thing!" ejaculated Tom. "A swim wouldn't go bad on such a hot day as this? Let us go in by all means!"

Sam was delighted at the suggestion, for the calm waters of the gulf looked very inviting. Dick did not care so much for a swim, but said he would go in if the others did.

"Dare vos a whole lot of pathing suits in von of der lockers," said Hans. "I vill git dem."

He soon appeared with the suits, and in less than ten minutes all of the boys were ready for a plunge. The waters of the gulf appeared to be unusually calm and nothing disturbed the surface.

"Here goes!" cried Tom, and poised on the rail he made a splendid dive and disappeared like a flash. Sam and Dick immediately followed. Hans remained on the rail, grinning.

"Why don't you come in, Hans?" yelled Sam, as he came up and commenced to swim about.

"I dink you vos chumps alretty," answered the German boy, calmly.

"Chumps?" returned Dick.

"Dot's it!"

"Why?"

"You chump oferpoard und you ton't know how you vos going to git pack, ain't it!" And now Hans laughed outright.

"Well, I never!" cried Tom. "We forgot to throw even a rope down!"

"We certainly would have had a time getting on deck," was Dick's comment. "Hans, throw an end of the rope ladder down."

"Dot vos vot I dink mineselluf," answered the German youth, and did as requested. Then he, too, took a dive, coming up and blowing like a porpoise.

It was certainly good sport and the four boys enjoyed it thoroughly. With the aid of the rope ladder it was easy to climb on the deck of the steam yacht, and they did a good deal of diving and running around. They also had a race, Tom offering a pint of ice cream to the first one around the ship. Dick won this race, with all of the others in a bunch at his heels. He was just reaching the end when Tom caught him by the ankle and held him fast.

"Hi, you! let go!" yelled Dick, and then turning, he promptly sent his brother downward, so that Tom had to let go.

"Wish I had a plate of ice cream," murmured Sam, when they were all resting on the rail of the steam yacht. "Wouldn't it be fine?"

"Oxactly," came from Hans. "Ven I gits me to a hotel again I vos order a plate a foot high, mit vanilla, strawperry, chocolate, orange ice, lemon—"

"Don't, Hans!" cried Tom, reproachfully. "You hurt my feelings so!" And with a comical grin he placed one hand over his stomach. "Just think of strawberry ice cream!"

"Or strawberries with cream! My, but it makes a fellow's mouth water!" came from Sam.

The boys remained in and out of the water the best part of two hours. It was so inviting all hated to think of dressing again. They had a game of tag and kept poor Hans "it" for a long while, until, in fact, the German youth was out of breath and had to give it up.

"I ton't run me no more, py golly!" panted Hans. "Of you vonts to been caught you caught yourselfs alretty!" And at this remark all of the others roared.

"I shouldn't mind our situation a bit if only we were certain the others were safe," remarked Dick, when they were dressing. "But when I think of Fred, Songbird, and Harold Bird—" He did not finish, but shook his head sorrowfully.

"It makes a fellow sick, doesn't it?" returned Sam. "Oh, I do hope they are safe!"

"I'll tell you one thing," came from Tom, walking up at this moment. "This swim has made me as hungry as a bear."

"Tom, did you ever know the time you weren't hungry?" demanded his elder brother.

"Sure," answered the fun-loving Rover, with a broad grin.

"When?" demanded both of the others.

"Directly after a good, square meal!" answered Tom, and then dodged hurriedly, to escape the shoe Dick hurled at him.

CHAPTER XIX

THE STORM ON THE GULF

"Boys, we are going to have a corker of a storm if ever there was one."

"I believe you, Dick. My, how the black clouds are rolling up!"

"And just when we were doing so nicely too."

The three Rover boys had come to the deck in a bunch, directly after the bath and a hearty meal.

It was Dick who had noticed the black clouds rolling up so suddenly and had called the attention of the others.

"How kvick der veader can change," sighed Hans. "Ven ve vos in schwimming I dink it vos lofely for a veek, ain't it!"

The boys had a good fire under the boiler and had tested the engine, to find it now in good working order. From one of the new joints the steam bubbled the least bit, but not sufficiently to do any harm or cause alarm. Dick had tried the wheel, to find it in the best of order. It thrilled him to take hold of the spokes and make the steam yacht answer to his will.

"I don't wonder some men wish to be pilots," he had said. "It's great to have a big steamer do just as you want her to." Then he had run the vessel around in the form of the figure 8, just to "get the knack of it," as he said.

"Shall we start for land in such a storm as this?" asked Sam. "It might drive us up on the rocks somewhere."

"We're a good way from land, Sam. Let us see what the storm will do first."

The black clouds increased rapidly, until the whole sky was overcast. Then a strong wind sprang up and the gulf was covered with whitecaps as far as the eye could reach.

"It's coming!" cried Sam, as the big raindrops began to fall. "We may as well get out of the wet."

"I think I'll run before the storm," said Dick. "We must either do that or face it. The yacht is beginning to roil."

"Yah, I feel dot!" sighed Hans, who had begun to turn pale.

"Hans, are you getting seasick?" demanded Sam.

"I ton't know, put I clink me my stomach vos going inside owid alretty!"

"You're certainly seasick," said Dick, with a grin. "Better lie down for a while."

"Oh, my!" groaned the German youth, and rushed, first to the rail of the steam yacht and then to the cabin. He was indeed sick, and that was the last the others saw of him while the storm lasted.

Soon came a whistling wind and then the rain fell in torrents. The sea was lashed into a white foam and the waves became higher and higher, crashing against the stern of the Mermaid, as she ran before them. At one moment the steam yacht would be on the top of the waves, the next she would sink down and down in the trough of the sea.

"You don't think we'll be wrecked, do you?" asked Sam, as he left his duty as fireman and came to the wheelhouse, where Dick stood, with all the windows down, trying to peer forth through the fury of the elements.

"Not at all, Sam,—but this is something fierce and no mistake."

"Poor Hans is down and out. I heard him rolling on his berth and groaning with distress."

"Well, leave him alone. He'll be sick as long as the storm lasts, most likely, and you'll only make matters worse by looking at him."

With the coming of night the storm appeared to increase. It was pitch-black on every side and Dick did not dare to run the Mermaid at more than quarter speed—just enough to keep her from swinging around broadside to the storm. All the lanterns were lit and hung up, Sam doing this with an oilsilk coat around him—a garment found in one of the staterooms. Yet he came in pretty wet.

"It's a screamer," he announced to Tom, as he dried himself by the boiler. "Never knew they could have such storms down here."

"They have storms all over the world," answered Tom. "What is Dick doing?"

"Running before the wind."

"He just told me to slow down more yet."

"Well, he can't see a thing ahead and he doesn't want to run into anything."

"And Hans?"

"Down, the sickest ever."

"Too bad! I know what it is to be sick. Better leave him alone."

"That's what Dick said."

As but little steam was needed Sam had no call to urge on his fire beneath the boiler, and he and Tom sat down near the speaking tube, to talk occasionally to Dick.

Thus two hours went by. Nobody had the least desire to go to sleep, even though the long swim had made each boy rather tired. The fury of the elements made them nervous.

"This puts me in mind of the time we were on the Pacific," called down Dick through the speaking tube. He referred to the adventures they had had as related in "The Rover Boys on Land and Sea."

"Well, we don't want to be cast away on a lonely island as we were then," said Sam.

"There are no islands around here," answered Tom. "I looked on the chart to make sure."

"In that case we can't hit anything. I am thinking—"

"Back her!" yelled Dick, through the speaking tube, and then jingled the bell.

Tom leaped for the engine and reversed it. There was a pause, and they felt the steam yacht swing half around. Then, after a wait, Dick ordered the speed ahead.

"What was wrong?" asked Tom, at the tube.

"Light right ahead," was the answer. "We cleared it by fifty feet. But I was scared, I can tell you that."

"What kind of a light?"

"A steamer—tramp, I reckon. She's way behind now."

Sam ran on deck to get a view of the stranger, but the fury of the storm shut out the sight.

"I suppose you didn't see much of her, Dick," he said, going into the wheelhouse.

"I saw enough," was the grim response. "I thought we were going to have a smashup sure, and I reckon the other pilot thought the same."

"Did you see anybody on board?"

"Not a soul. She came up like a ghost, with only two lights showing, and by the time I had backed and turned she was gone. But it nearly gave me nervous collapse," added the amateur pilot.

The wind was now so heavy that it sent the rain against the pilot house in solid sheets. Dick could not see ahead at all and he requested Sam to go to the bow, to keep the best lookout possible.

"If you see anything wrong yell to me," he said. "And be careful that you don't tumble overboard." And then he spoke to Tom through the tube and asked the amateur engineer to play fireman also for the time being.

Wrapped in the raincoat, and with a cap pulled far down over his head, Sam took up his station near the bow, clinging to the rail for protection. He knew their safety depended in good part on keeping a sharp lookout and he eyed the darkness ahead closely. So far there had been little lightning and scarcely any thunder, but now the rumbling increased until there came a crash and a flare that made all on the Mermaid jump.

"Did that hit us?" yelled Tom up the tube.

"No, but it was pretty close," answered Dick,

"Where is Sam now?"

"At the forward rail. I can see nothing from the wheelhouse."

"If it gets much worse you had better come below and let the boat run itself, Dick."

"I can't do that, Tom—I must stick to my post."

Another half-hour went by, and there was no let up in the fury of the storm. Poor Sam was almost exhausted and, tying the wheel fast for the time being, Dick went to him.

"Better come in," he said. "If you'll take the wheel I'll stay out here. Just keep her straight before the storm."

"All right," panted poor Sam, and made his way back to the wheel-house step by step, and holding on to whatever was handy, to keep from being swept overboard.

Sam had interested himself in steering from the start and knew how to handle a wheel moderately well. He looked at the compass and saw that they were running almost due east, varying a little to the southward. He untied the wheel and kept to the course with but little trouble.

"Dick has gone on the lookout," he explained to Tom. And then he added: "You've got the best job to-night."

"I'd come up, if you could run the engine," was Tom's reply.

"No, you had better attend to that, Tom."

"Doesn't the storm seem to be letting up?"

"Not a particle. If anything it is growing worse."

"It must be a hurricane."

"It is—or next door to it," answered the youngest of the Rovers.

The thunder and lightning appeared to draw closer, until the steam yacht was literally surrounded by the electrical display. The flashes of lightning were so blinding that, for the moment afterward, neither Sam nor Dick could see anything. Sam tried to keep the windows of the pilot house fairly clean, but the effort was a dismal failure.

Presently came one awful flash and crash that caused Sam to sink back in a heap on one of the pilot-house cushions. He felt that the steam yacht must have been struck and every nerve in his body tingled and quivered. Only after a strong effort was he able to pull himself together and clutch the wheel once more.

"Dick must have felt that," he murmured. "I wish—"

Another flash of lightning, but less vivid, interrupted his meditations. He looked out of the front window towards where Dick had been standing. Then he gave a cry of alarm.

His big brother had disappeared!

CHAPTER XX

A NIGHT OF ANXIETY

Had the lightning struck Dick and knocked him overboard?

Such was the terrifying question which Sam asked himself as he stared out of the pilothouse window into the darkness before him. Another flash of lightning lit up the scene and he made certain that his big brother was nowhere in sight.

"Tom! Tom!" he yelled down the tube, frantically.

"What now, Sam?"

"Dick is gone—struck by lightning, I guess. Come up!"

At this alarming information Tom left the engine room at a bound and came on deck almost as soon as it can be told. He met Sam running toward the bow.

"Where was Dick?" he screamed, to make himself heard above the roaring and shrieking of the wind.

"At the forward rail, on the lookout. He was standing there just before that awful crash came, and I haven't seen him since."

No more was said by either, but holding fast to whatever came to hand, the two Rovers worked their way forward until they reached the rail where Dick had been standing. They now saw that the fore-topmast had come down, hitting the rail and breaking it loose for a distance of several feet.

"The mast must have hit Dick and knocked him overboard," said Tom, with a quiver in his voice.

"Oh, Tom!" Sam could say no more, but his heart sank.

The two boys stared around helplessly, not knowing what to do. Dick was very dear to them and they could not bear to think that he was lost, and forever.

Suddenly, as another flash of lightning lit up the scene, Sam caught sight of something dark lying just a few feet away. He rushed over, to see Dick lying in a heap, his head under his forearm.

"Dick! Dick!" he cried. "Are you killed?"

There was no answer, and now both Tom and Sam knelt beside their brother and raised him up. His face was pale and the blood was flowing from a cut over the left temple.

"The topmast hit him when it came down," said Tom. "Let us carry him to the cabin."

They raised their brother up and, not without difficulty, took him to the companionway and down to the cabin. Here they placed him on the couch and Sam got some water and bathed his wounded forehead. They saw he was not dead but unconscious from the blow received.

"I must look to the engine,—I don't want the Mermaid to blow up," said Tom, and rushed off,—to get back in less than three minutes. By this time Dick was gasping and groaning, and soon he opened his eyes.

"Dick," said Sam, softly. "Don't worry, you are safe."

"Sam! Th—the mast came down on m—me!"

"We know it. We found you in a heap on the deck. I was afraid you had been knocked overboard. It was that awful flash of lightning did it, I think."

"Yes."

Dick could say little more just then and did not try. Sam and Tom made him as comfortable as possible and found he had suffered only from the fall of the topmast and not the lightning stroke itself.

"If Hans felt a little better he might look after Dick, but he is still as sick as ever," said Tom. "He declares we are all going to the bottom and he doesn't care if we do!"

"That's the way with folks who are real seasick," answered Sam. "They feel so utterly miserable they don't care what happens."

Leaving Dick on the couch in the cabin, Sam returned to the wheelhouse and Tom to the engine room. The steam yacht had been drifting and the waves were dashing over a portion of her deck. As quickly as possible Sam brought the craft around and now headed her up to the storm, which made her ride better than ever.

For some reason neither Sam nor Tom thought of the disagreeableness of the situation after that. Both were overjoyed to think that Dick had escaped serious injury. The foretopmast lay on the forward deck still, but as it was not in the way it was allowed to remain there for the time being.

Thus the whole of the night wore away, and with the coming of morning the storm gradually died down. But the waves still ran high and it was noon ere the sun came out, to cheer them up.

"I am thankful that is over," said Sam, breathing a deep sigh of relief. "I never want to go through such a night again."

"Nor I," answered Tom. "It takes all the fun out of a chap."

Dick got up, a handkerchief tied around his forehead. He still felt a trifle weak but that was all.

"I will take the wheel," he said to Sam. "If you want to do something you can get breakfast—and be sure and make plenty of hot coffee, for we need it to make us less sleepy."

As the storm went down, Hans came forth from his stateroom, pale and so woebegone that Tom had to turn away to hide a smile.

"Vos dot storm ofer alretty?" asked Hans, sinking in a chair.

"Just about," answered Dick.

"Oh, such a night, Dick! I ton't forgot him of I lif a dousand years, ain't it!"

"We shan't forget it either, Hans."

"Dick, I durn me insides owit more as fifty dimes, yes!" went on the German youth, earnestly.

"We've had our own troubles too," said the eldest Rover, and then related what had occurred. Hans was glad Dick had escaped falling overboard but was still too weak to take a great deal of interest.

The wheel was lashed fast and the engine slowed down, and all hands went to breakfast. It was by no means an elaborate meal, yet it made all but Hans feel much better. The German youth had little appetite and ate sparingly.

"Der kvicker ve git py land on der besser vill I like him," said he.

"Maybe you won't be seasick after such a dose," said Sam, hopefully.

During the night all of the Rovers had become more or less soaked and they were anxious to find a complete change of clothing, so that their own might be thoroughly dried.

"Sam, you can hunt around for some things," said Dick. "I'll go back to the wheel and you, Tom, had better go back to the engine. Hans, will you help Sam?"

"Sure I vill dot," answered the German boy.

Sam knew where there were several lockers containing both outer clothing and underwear and he proceeded to these, followed by Hans. They soon had one locker open and hauled forth what it contained.

"This underwear will about fit Dick and Tom," he said. "It's rather big for me, though."

"Vell, maype der udder closets got someding schmaller in dem," suggested Hans, and opened up a second locker.

Here they found a variety of things, including socks, shoes, collars, cuffs, and even fancy neckties.

"Whoever was on board of this steam yacht left everything behind him when he went away," was the comment of the youngest Rover.

They next opened a locker filled with outer clothing, including linen coats and panama hats. As the weather was growing warmer this just suited the boys.

"Hello, here is a pretty big suit," observed Sam, hauling it forth and holding it up. "The man who wore that must have been a pretty large fellow. Even Dick would get lost in that suit."

"Dot's so!" exclaimed Hans. "Vait, I try on dot coats. Ha! Ha! Ain't he schmall alretty!" And Hans began to roar, for the coat came to his knees and the sleeves hid his hands from sight.

"You've got to grow, Hans, before you can fill that," said Sam, laughing.

"Vell, maype I grow some day."

"You will if you eat plenty of sauerkraut and Limburger cheese," and Sam grinned broadly.

"I vos eat vot I blease, Sam Rofer!"

Hans took off the coat and in doing so turned the garment over. From out of one of the pockets there fell a flat cardcase of red morocco leather.

"Hello, you've dropped something, Hans."

"So I tit," answered the German youth, and flinging aside the coat he picked up the leather cardcase.

"Has it got any cards in it?" questioned Sam, with sudden interest.

"Dot vos vot I vos going to see. Now vait, I vill oben him," went on Hans, backing away as the youngest Rover reached out for the case.

"Well, do hurry, Hans! You are so slow!" cried Sam, impatiently.

"Vot's der use of hurrying ven you got lots of dime, hey?"

"I want to see what is in the case."

"Maype der tont been noddings in him."

"Hans, will you open it, please?"

"Yah."

"Well, then, do so."

With great deliberation the German youth opened the leather cardcase. Out of it fluttered a small card photograph. Sam picked it up, gave one look, and let out a cry of astonishment.

"Well, I never!"

CHAPTER XXI

THE PICTURE IN THE CARDCASE

"Who is it?" questioned Hans, trying to gain possession of the photograph, but instead of answering Sam started from the cabin.

"I must show this to Dick and Tom!" he cried. "Come along."

"Yah, put—" began the German boy, and then stopped, for there was nobody to talk to, Sam being already out of sight.

"Dick, look what I found," cried the youngest Rover, as he dashed into the pilot house.

"A fortune?" asked Dick, with a smile.

"No, a picture. Just look!"

Dick did as requested and gave a start.

"You found this on the yacht?" he cried. "Yes. In the pocket of a big coat hanging in one of the lockers. It was in a cardcase."

"This is certainly queer. It looks exactly like Harold Bird, doesn't it?"

"It certainly is Harold. I wonder—Oh, look!"

Sam had turned the picture over. On the back were these words, written in a strong, masculine hand:

To father, from Harold. Merry Xmas!

"Why, Harold must have given this to his father," said Dick, thoughtfully.—"And if so—"

"Do you think the coat belonged to Mr. Bird?" broke in Sam.

"Perhaps. Did you find anything else?"

"Ve titn't look," came from Hans, who stood in the doorway. "So dot vos a picture of Harold Pird, alretty! Dot vos kveer!"

"It is astonishing," said Dick. "Sam, see if you can find anything else."

Sam went back and Hans with him, and while they were gone

Dick, through the speaking tube, acquainted Tom with the discovery made.

"Maybe Mr. Bird was on this steam yacht," called up Tom.

Sam and Hans went over the stuff in the lockers with care. They found some cards bearing the name of James Morrison and a short note about a meeting of a yacht club addressed to Barton Knox.

"Those men must have been on the Mermaid," said Sam. "Perhaps they were part owners. Frequently several men or a whole club own a yacht like this in common."

"Vell, she ton't vos a common poat," was Hans' comment. "She vos a peauty."

Sam was on the point of giving up the search when he saw something sticking from a crack next to the wall. He pulled the object forth and saw it was the photograph of a big, heavy-set man with rather a handsome face. He turned it over and gave a short gasp, for on the back was written in pencil:

Sharwell Lee Bird, Murderer.

"What a horrible thing to write!" murmured the youngest Rover. "It makes a fellow shiver to read it!"

"Of he killed dot man ven he vos hunting he vos sure a murderer, Sam."

"Not exactly, Hans; he didn't mean to shoot the fellow. It was accidental."

"Yah, put der mans vos teat, ain't it!"

"Yes, and the death of the poor fellow drove Mr. Bird insane. I must show this to Dick, and to Tom, too."

Sam took the second picture, and all on board the steam yacht discussed the discovery for some time. But they could reach no conclusion saving that Mr. Bird had likely been on the vessel at one time and had left his coat and the two pictures behind him.

"Perhaps he was on this vessel after he disappeared from Kingston," said Tom. "If so, the question is, Where did he go after that?"

"We must tell Harold of this, the first chance we get," said Sam.

"Providing he is alive," answered Dick. "Remember, we are not at all sure that the Mascotteoutlived that crash in the fog."

The middle of the afternoon found the Mermaid steaming on her course at a good rate of speed. Tom had now become fairly familiar with the engine and he allowed the steam to run up some pounds higher than before. Hans fell to tending the fire and Sam took turns with Dick at the wheel.

"We ought to sight some kind of land by to-morrow," said the eldest Rover. "But of course there is no telling where we will fetch up, exactly."

"Somewhere on the coast of Florida, and not very many miles from Tampa Bay, I reckon," returned Sam. "By the way, Dick, don't you think the rascals on the Dogstar have had ample time in which to make their escape?"

"Perhaps so. But the storm may have crippled them, and we may overtake them even yet. A sailing vessel can't make the speed a steamer or a steam yacht can."

Twice during the afternoon they saw vessels at a distance, one a steamer and the other a bark, and both bound westward. Neither came close enough to be hailed and our friends did not think it wise to raise any signals of distress.

"The yacht is running all right now," said Dick. "We may as well take her into port and get the salvage money. The amount will be a good round sum."

"Do you know, I shouldn't mind owning a steam yacht like this myself," said Tom, to whom he was speaking. "Couldn't we take some dandy trips, off the coast of New England and elsewhere!"

"We certainly could, Tom. But you must remember that we ought to go back to school. If we don't, we'll never get through. It's about time I was thinking of college."

"I hate to think of leaving Putnam Hall, Dick. Why, the place is just like a second home to me!"

"It is to all of us. But we are growing older and must either go to college or get into business."

The sun was setting when Dick went on deck again. Hans was preparing supper and Sam was at his station in the pilot house. The waters of the gulf were growing calm and the scene was a beautiful one.

"This is something like," remarked the eldest Rover, as he drew in a deep breath of fresh air. "Doesn't look like the storm of last night, eh, Sam?"

"No, Dick, this is just splendid."

"What's that ahead?" asked the big brother, casting his eye on a dark speck directly in the track of the steam yacht.

"I don't know—I didn't see it before."

The object, whatever it was, was a long way ahead, and by the time they drew closer it was too dark to see clearly. But Dick saw enough to make him cry out in astonishment:

"A rowboat, and full of men!"

The eldest Rover was indeed right, it was a large rowboat and it contained six persons, four of whom were at the oars and the others in the stern. The rowboat contained in addition a keg of water and several small boxes and tins.

"Ship ahoy!" came hoarsely over the water, as the steam yacht drew closer to the small craft.

"Ahoy!" called back Dick, and ran forward, while Sam signaled to Tom to stop the engine.

"Can you take us on board?" was the question from a man in the rowboat. "We've lost our ship and we are played out."

"Certainly we can take you on board," answered Dick. "Wait a minute, and I'll throw you a rope ladder."

"Thank you very much!" called back the man.

The steam yacht was brought to a standstill and the ladder thrown out. Soon the rowboat came tip to the ladder, and one after another those aboard the small craft mounted to the deck of the

Mermaid. The three Rovers and Hans were at hand to see who they were.

"Dan Baxter!"

"Sack Todd!"

Such were the cries that came from Sam and Tom. Two of the new arrivals were indeed the persons named, and a third was Gasper Pold.

"Did you come from the Dogstar?" demanded Dick.

"We did," answered Dan Baxter, sullenly. Evidently he was much chagrined over this unexpected meeting.

"Have you been following us in this steam yacht?" asked Sack Todd, with a sickly grin on his hard face.

"We were certainly following you," answered Tom. "But we didn't start out in this vessel. We—"

"Tom!" said Dick, warningly, and then Tom shut up instantly.

"Who's the captain here?" demanded one of the men from the rowboat.

"I suppose I am, for the present," answered Dick.

"You!" And the man, a burly fellow, took a step back in astonishment.

"Yes. Who are you?"

"I am Sid Jeffers, first mate of the Dogstar. We sprung several bad leaks in that storm last night and made up our mind the schooner was going down. So we got out the boats and I and two men and these three chaps manned one of them. We lost sight of the ship in the dark,—and here we are. We're mighty hungry and we'd like something to eat. And if you've got any liquor on board let us have it by all means," concluded Sid Jeffers.

CHAPTER XXII

AN UNEXPECTED MEETING ON THE WATER

It was plainly to be seen that the first mate of the Dogstar was in no wise an agreeable person to meet, and the Rovers and Hans were sorry that he and the others had come aboard the steam yacht. The two sailors from the lumber schooner were also rough men and probably under the thumb of the mate.

"We can give you what is on board of the Mermaid," said Dick, a little stiffly. "I have not looked for liquor, so I can't say if there is any on the vessel or not."

"Captain, and don't know what's aboard!" exclaimed Sid Jeffers.

While he was speaking Sack Todd and Dan Baxter had been looking around the deck in the semi-darkness.

"Where are the rest of the people on this boat?" demanded the ex-counterfeiter.

"I don't see anybody," declared Dan Baxter. "Say, do you know what I think?" he cried suddenly. "I think these fellows are all alone!"

"Humph!" muttered Sack Todd. "If they are—" He did not finish, but smiled quietly to himself.

"Where can we get something to eat?" demanded the first mate, after a rather awkward pause.

"In the galley or the cabin, as you please," said Dick. "But you will have to prepare it yourselves. We have no cook on board."

"Oh, that's it, eh? Well, Guirk can cook pretty good and he can do the trick for us, eh, Guirk?"

"Aye, aye!" answered one of the sailors. "Just show me the victuals an' the stove, an' I'll be after doing the rest in jig time. I'm hungry enough to eat 'most anything."

Dick led the way to the galley and the crowd from the small boat followed; one sailor stopping long enough to tie the rowboat astern.

"Nobody else on board, eh?" said Sid Jeffers, turning suddenly on Dick.

"No, not at present," answered the eldest Rover, boldly.

"Where are you bound?"

"For Tampa Bay."

"What vessel is this?"

"The steam yacht Mermaid."

"Did you charter her?"

"No, we found her," answered Dick, resolved to tell the plain truth.

"Found her?" came from the mate and also from Dan Baxter.

"Yes."

"Where?"

"Out here in the gulf."

"Who was on board?" questioned Sack Todd.

"Nobody."

"Nobody!" came from all the newcomers.

"Do you mean to say there wasn't a soul on this boat when you found her?" asked Dan Baxter, in high curiosity.

"That is the truth," said Tom. "She was drifting around, abandoned. We simply climbed on board and took possession."

"Out in the middle of the gulf?" asked the first mate, incredulously.

"Yes."

"Ve vos shipwrecked and vos mighty glad to got on board," said Hans.

"Oh, that's it!" cried Sid Jeffers and a gleam of intelligence shot from his eyes. "Mighty lucky you was, and no error! A ship like this is worth a pile of money. But let us have something to eat and to drink first and then we can talk matters over. A fellow can't pow-wow well on an empty stomach."

He spoke a few words in a low tone to his two men and they

passed into the galley, where Hans and Sam showed them the food that was on board. In the meantime Sid Jeffers went on a hunt for liquor, and finding a bottle took a long drink, and then passed it over to Sack Todd and the others.

"Dick, I don't like this at all," whispered Tom, as soon as he could get the chance.

"Neither do I, Tom. I never expected to meet this crowd out here."

"There are six of them, while we number only four," went on the fun-loving Rover.

"Come with me," answered Dick, softly. "Sam, you take charge for a while," he added to his youngest brother.

Dick led the way to the main cabin of the Mermaid and to a case which was screwed fast to the wall. Inside were several pistols, and below were several boxes of ammunition.

"I reckon I understand you," said Tom. "We had better arm ourselves at once. There is no telling what those fellows will take it into their heads to do."

"Let us four arm ourselves, and then hide all the other pistols," said Dick. "Then, if they are not armed, we'll have them at something of a disadvantage."

They took four pistols,—one for Sam and another for Hans,—with the necessary cartridges, and then all of the remaining weapons were hidden at the bottom of one of the berths. This accomplished they went on deck again, and called Sam and Hans.

"They are having a big time, eating and drinking," said Sam, as he took the weapon handed to him. "I feel sure we will have trouble sooner or later. Pold, Todd, and Baxter won't want to run the risk of being arrested as soon as we land, and that mate and his men may side with them."

"That isn't the only thing," said Dick. "They know this steam yacht is valuable. The party to bring the vessel in to port will get big money. Didn't the mate speak of it? That shows how his mind was running."

Our friends talked the matter over for some time, but the conversation did not relieve their worry. They felt that there was serious trouble ahead of them and that it might break out at any moment.

"You know the old school whistle," said Dick. "If anybody gets into trouble whistle, and then the others can come to his aid." And so it was agreed.

Not knowing what else to do, Dick went to the pilot house followed by Hans, while Tom returned to the engine room and Sam to his job as fireman. Soon the engine was started up once more, and the steam yacht headed again for the western coast of Florida. It proved to be a clear night, and though there was no moon the stars shone brightly in the heavens.

A full hour went by, during which time the party from the Dogstar made themselves at home aboard the Mermaid. They feasted on the best the steam yacht afforded and several of the men drank a good-deal of liquor.

"This is like falling into the softest kind of a snap," declared Sack Todd, after he and Gasper Pold had been talking in a corner for some time. "They don't own this steam yacht any more than we do."

"Right you are," answered the other.

"And if they calculate to take us to Tampa and hand us over to the officers of the law, why—"

"Not much, Todd! I am not going to prison just yet."

"Can you trust Jeffers? You seem to know him pretty well."

"I think I can. Jeffers is close—he likes money—and he sees big money in this steam yacht."

"That's an idea! Now what of the two sailors?"

"I think Guirk and the other fellow will do what the first mate tells them to—especially if he promises them good wages for the job."

"And what of Baxter? Remember, he used to go to school with the Rovers."

"I don't know what to make of him. Sometimes I think he is all right, and then again I don't feel like trusting him."

"That's my way of it, too. We don't want anybody we can't trust in this."

"Oh, he'll have to do as we say."

"Hello, what's up there?" shouted Sid Jeffers, from the bench where he was sitting, finishing some liquor before him.

"We want to talk certain things over," said Gasper Pold. "Come here."

In a cautious manner Sack Todd and Gasper Pold "sounded" the first mate of the ill-fated Dogstar. They said, if they could get control of the steam yacht, it might mean big money to all concerned.

"But what will you do with those Rover boys and the Dutch lad?" asked Jeffers.

"Oh, we can either cast them adrift somewhere or else put them off on a deserted shore," answered Sack Todd. "Then I can turn this steam yacht over to a friend of mine—an utter stranger to them—and he can get the salvage on the craft for us and we can divide up."

This plan to make money appealed strongly to the first mate, and he finally agreed to aid the others in gaining possession of the craft. Then the two sailors were instructed by Jeffers and they agreed to do as ordered, leaving the consequences on the mate's shoulders. Finally Dan Baxter was consulted.

"I don't care what you do, so long as we can get away from the officers of the law," said the bully. "But don't kill anybody—I won't stand for that," he added, showing that his hard heart had at least one soft spot in it.

CHAPTER XXIII

THE ENEMY TRIES TO TAKE POSSESSION

"Say, boy, come down in the cabin; I want to talk to you."

It was Sack Todd who spoke and he addressed Hans, who had left the pilot house to look over the stern, to see if the rowboat was still safe.

"Vot you vonts of me?" asked Hans, in surprise.

"I want to ask you a few questions," returned Todd, smoothly.

Hans was a trifle suspicious, and yet he saw no direct reason for refusing to comply with Sack Todd's request. He followed the ex-counterfeiter across the deck and down the companionway.

"I want to ask your opinion of this letter," said Sack Todd, as he laid a written sheet on the table. "We can't understand it at all. I know you are a pretty smart boy and maybe you can help us."

Flattered by the compliment paid him, the German youth took up the letter and scanned it by the light of the swinging lamp. As he did so, Sack Todd closed the cabin door and motioned to Gasper Pold and Dan Baxter, who stood behind an angle of the wall.

Almost before he could realize it, poor Hans was a prisoner. His arms were held tightly by someone, while someone else thrust a gag into his mouth and fastened it by means of a cloth running to the back of his neck.

"Sthop! ton't choke me!" he gasped, and that was all he was allowed to utter. Then his arms were fastened, and his feet secured.

"Now, into the stateroom with him!" cried Gasper Pold, and the three evildoers lifted the prisoner up, carried him into one of the staterooms, and threw him on the berth. Then the door was closed and locked.

"That's Number One," declared Sack Todd. "And an easy job, too."

"If you can bag the others as easily, it will be a grand job," was Dan Baxter's comment.

"We must get one of those chaps up from below next," said Gasper Pold. "Baxter, you can go down and tell one of them his brother in the wheelhouse wants to see him. We'll catch him on the stairs."

"All right," said the former bully of Putnam Hall.

He hurried down to the engine room and then to the nearest coal bunker, where Sam was shoveling coal.

"Sam!" he called out, to make himself heard.

"Hullo, Dan Baxter, what do you want?"

"Dick wants you on deck at once."

"What for?"

"I don't know—I think Hans has a fit. That Dutch boy always was a queer stick," muttered Dan Baxter.

"All right, I'll go up," answered the youngest Rover, and dropping his shovel, he hurried through the engine room.

"Sam!" called Tom, warningly, but his brother did not hear him on account of the noise made by the machinery.

All unconscious of the trap laid for him, poor Sam started to go on deck, when he was hurled backward in a dark corner of a passageway. Somebody came down on top of him, a gag was forced into his mouth, and a rope was brought into use.

"Let—let up!" he managed to say. "Help!" And then his wind was completely cut off for the moment until the gag was secured.

But though gagged the youngest Rover was game and did not give up. He squirmed and kicked and landed a blow on Gasper Pold and another on Dan Baxter. In return the former bully of Putnam Hall kicked him in the side, and then the men tied him up, hands and feet.

"Where will you put him?" asked Baxter.

"Put him in another of the staterooms,—for the present," answered Sack Todd. "After we have got them all we can put them somewhere else."

"Shall we search him?" went on Dan Baxter, who was anxious to know what Sam might be carrying.

"Not now—we haven't time."

Poor Sam was placed in a stateroom next to that occupied by Hans, and then the evildoers hurried off to see what they could do in the way of capturing Dick. They expected to take the eldest Rover unawares, but in this they were mistaken.

In the meantime, Tom, full of suspicion from the very start, called up the speaking tube to his brother.

"I say, Dick, what's the mater with Dutchy?"

"Hans? Nothing that I know of," returned Dick. "Why?"

"Dan Baxter was just down here and said you wanted Sam quick —that something was wrong with Hans."

"I didn't send for Sam!" cried Dick, excitedly. He looked around him in the gloom. "Hans isn't here," he went on, down the tube.

"Well, look out—I think something is wrong," shouted back Tom. "Got your pistol handy?"

Dick felt in his pocket, and found the weapon where he had placed it. Then he looked around again, but the deck of the Mermaid appeared to be deserted.

"I'm going to see what has become of Sam!" he shouted down the tube. "I'll tie the wheel fast."

"Keep out of trouble!" shouted back Tom. "If I don't hear from you pretty quick I'll be up myself," he added.

With his hand on his pistol, Dick left the wheelhouse and walked slowly and cautiously toward the waist of the steam yacht. As he rounded a corner of the cabin he heard a murmur of voices, and the next moment he found himself confronted by Pold, Todd, the mate of the Dogstar, and Dan Baxter.

The evildoers were taken somewhat by surprise and halted in confusion. In the semi-darkness Dick saw that one carried a gag and cloth and the two others ropes.

"There he is!" faltered Dan Baxter, before he had time to think.

"No, you don't!" cried Dick, stepping back several paces. "What were you going to do?" he demanded.

"We want to talk to you," answered Sack Todd, smoothly.

"What do you want? Stand back! I don't want any of you to come closer."

"See here, Mr. Rover, it's all right," came from Gasper Pold. "We ain't going to harm you. We only want to have a little peaceable palaver."

"Where is my brother Sam? And where is Hans Mueller?"

"They are both in the cabin. I was going to ask you to join us, in a general talk," said Sack Todd, catching his cue from Gasper Pold as to how best to proceed.

"We want to find out where you are taking us," put in the mate of the Dogstar.

"You are acting very queerly," said Dick. He had backed up close to one of the small cabin windows, which was open. "Sam! Hans!" he yelled suddenly, and at the top of his lungs.

Of course there was no reply, and satisfied that something was indeed wrong he retreated still further.

"Stop him!" yelled Gasper Pold. "Don't let him get below to where his brother is!"

He meant Tom, and Dick instantly made up his mind that the best thing he could do would be to get to the engine room and warn his fun-loving brother of their peril. He made a turn, sent Sack Todd and Dan Baxter sprawling, and an instant later was diving out of sight down the ladder leading to the machinery.

"Dick! I thought something was wrong and I was coming up!" came from Tom. "What of Sam and Hans?"

"I don't know. They are after me! Have you your pistol?"

"Yes, and I'll use it too, if they bother me," answered Tom, determinedly.

"Stop where you are!" cried Dick, looking up the iron ladder. "My brother and I have pistols and we shall use them if you attempt to follow down here!"

"Look out!" yelled Dan Baxter, in alarm, and tumbled back to a safe place. "They'll shoot sure, I know 'em!"

At these words all at the top of the iron ladder hesitated. In the meantime both Tom and Dick held their pistols up, so that the shining barrels could be dimly seen.

"They are armed, hang the luck!" muttered Sack Todd. "And they tell me they can shoot, too!"

"Look here, we don't want any shooting," said Gasper Pold. "We want this affair conducted peaceable-like."

"I know what you want," said Tom, boldly. "You want to make us prisoners."

"Like as not Sam and Hans are already prisoners," said Dick. "If they were not we'd surely hear something from them."

"They are prisoners," answered Dan Baxter.

"And you might as well give in. It won't do you any good to hold out—we are six to two, remember."

"Baxter, did you plan this?" asked Tom.

"Oh, I'm not saying who planned it. We have simply made up our minds to take command of the steam yacht, that's all."

"The yacht was a derelict," put in Sid Jeffers. "We have as much right to her as you have."

"Not at all—we found her," answered Dick.

"But you couldn't have brought her safely in to port," put in Gasper Pold. "We are going to do that—and get the salvage money," he added, triumphantly.

CHAPTER XXIV

IN THE ENGINE ROOM

After the bold declaration of Gasper Pold there was an awkward pause. Dick and Tom did not know what to do and neither did the party at the top of the engineroom ladder.

"Are you going to give in or not?" demanded Sack Todd, at length.

"Why should we give in?" asked Dick.

"Because if you do, we'll treat you well."

"And if we don't—" came from Tom.

"Then you'll have to take the consequences. As Baxter says, we are six to two, so it is all nonsense for you to think you can hold out against us."

"Supposing we do give in, what are you going to do with us?" asked Dick, curiously but with no present intention of submitting to the evildoers.

"Oh, we'll treat you fairly enough," put in Gasper Pold. "We'll give you all you want to eat and drink and put you off at some safe place along the coast."

"Come, do you submit?" demanded the mate of the Dogstar.

"What do you say, Dick?" whispered Tom, so faintly that the others could not hear.

"I don't want to give in to them."

"Neither do I. But it looks pretty shaky, doesn't it?"

"Yes, they have us cornered."

"We are armed, and if there is to be any shooting we can do our share of it," resumed Sack Todd. "But there is no need to go to such an extreme. Better submit quietly and let that end it. We wish you no harm, but we are bound to have our way."

"Let Sam and Hans come down and we'll talk it over," said Dick, struck by a sudden idea.

"You had better come up, and then you can talk it over in the cabin," said Sack Todd, and whispered something to his companion the Rovers could not hear.

"Not yet," said Dick, firmly.

"All right, suit yourself. But if you won't come up, you can stay there. Throw over the hatch, fellows."

There was a hatch to fit over the opening to the engine room and without further words this was thrown into place and secured from the deck.

"Dick, we are prisoners!" cried Tom.

"It certainly looks like it," answered the eldest Rover, soberly. "There is another door,—but it is locked from the other side, I think."

They listened and heard the men and Baxter walk away from the hatchway. Then all became quiet, for Tom had stopped the engine.

For over half an hour the two Rover boys remained in the engine room of the Mermaid doing little but walk around. With the hatch closed it was very hot down there, and Dick, who had his coat on, was glad to discard that garment. They could get little or no fresh air, and both wondered how long they could stand the confinement.

"I wouldn't care so much, if only I knew Sam and Hans were safe," remarked Dick. "But for all we know, they may have been killed."

"Oh, I don't think that," answered his brother. "I don't think Dan Baxter is quite so wicked."

Presently there came a noise above and the hatch was raised. The next instant Sam came tumbling down the iron ladder, followed by Hans.

"Now you fellows can talk it over as long as you like," said Gasper Pold. "When you come to terms let us know by blowing the steam whistle."

And then the hatch was put down and fastened as before.

"Sam, are you all right?" asked Dick and Tom, in a breath.

"Oh, yes, after a fashion," answered the youngest Rover. "But they handled me pretty roughly."

"And you, Hans?"

"I dink I vos peen putty vell hammered alretty. Py chimanatics! I vish I could drow dem all oferpoard, ain't it!"

"We are in a box, in more ways than one," said Tom.

"What did they do to you?" questioned Dick, and then Sam and Hans told their stories, adding that they had been taken from the staterooms but a few minutes before, brought on deck, unbound and ungagged, and sent down the iron ladder as already mentioned.

"I was afraid first they were going to throw us overboard," said Sam. "I think Sack Todd is equal to it, and that Gasper Pold is about as bad."

The four youths talked the situation over for a good hour, but could reach no satisfactory conclusion. They did not wish to submit to the others and yet they realized that they were "in a box" as Tom said.

"I know one thing—I want a drink of water," said Sam. "I am as dry as a salt fish."

"Yah, I vont me a trink, too," added Hans.

"Well, you'll have to go without," answered Tom. "I am dry myself. I was going to get some fresh water just before the trouble began, but I didn't have the chance."

"I know what they'll do—they'll starve us out," exclaimed Sam. "I see their game plainly."

"I am going to whistle for water," said Tom, with something of his usual grin. "Nothing like being stylish."

He pulled the cord and the whistle gave a loud toot. He repeated this several times, when they heard footsteps and the hatch was raised about a foot.

"Ready to submit?" asked Sack Todd, peering down on them.

"We want some drinking water," answered Tom.

"Oh, pshaw!" said the man, in disgust.

"Will you give us a bucket of fresh water or not?' asked Dick.

"Maybe—I'll see," said Todd, and dropped the hatch into place once more.

"I don't believe he'll give us a thing," was Sam's comment. "He knows if he doesn't we'll have to give up sooner or later."

"Of ve only had apout two dozen policemans here!" sighed the German youth.

In the meanwhile Sack Todd told the others about the water.

"Are you going to give it to them?" questioned Dan Baxter.

"Don't think I will," was the answer.

"You can't let them die of thirst," went on the former bully of Putnam Hall, with some little show of feeling.

"I've got an idea," came from Gasper Pold. "Is there a medicine cabinet on board? Generally such a vessel carries one."

"Yes, there is one in the cabin," answered Sid Jeffers. "What do you want of it?"

"We might put some dope in the drinking water. That will fix 'em."

"What, you wouldn't poison them!" cried Dan Baxter, and gave a little shiver.

"Oh, we'll only put them to sleep," answered Gasper Pold, but with a look on his face that Baxter did not like.

The men went to the cabin and the former bully of Putnam Hall followed. Here the medicine cabinet was found filled with various liquids and powders and Gasper Pold looked them over with care.

"I worked in a drug store when I was a young man," he explained. "And I took a good bit of interest in dopes and poisons."

Dan Baxter heard him say this, and to the credit of the bully it made him shudder. He was no friend to the Rovers, yet he did not wish to see them lose their lives. He paused for a moment, then turned and ran on deck.

Nobody was in sight, for the sailors from the Dogstar were asleep below. He ran for a bucket, filled it with water and took it to the hatchway, which he opened feverishly.

"Hullo there!" he whispered.

"Baxter, is it you?" queried Dick, coming to the ladder.

"Yes. Take this bucket of water, quick. It's clean and good. Don't drink what the others bring you."

"But, Baxter—" began Tom.

"I can't stay. Be careful of what they give you to eat and drink, that's all." And the next moment the bucket was passed to Dick, the hatch closed down, and Baxter fairly ran back to where he had left the men.

"What can this mean?" asked Dick, staring at his companions.

"Dick, be careful," warned Sam. "It may be some plot of Baxter's."

"Maype ve ton't besser trink dot vater," suggested Hans. "I ton't vont to vake up teat in der morning, ain't it!"

"Can the water be poisoned?" asked Tom.

They poured some in a glass and held it close to the light. It looked good and Dick tasted it cautiously.

"Baxter said to beware of what the others gave us to eat and to drink," said Sam. "Evidently something is in the air."

All sniffed of the water and tasted it, yet each was afraid to take a regular drink. While they were deliberating they heard the hatch being raised again. Then Sack Todd and Gasper Pold appeared once more.

CHAPTER XXV

ONE PLOT AND ANOTHER

"We've got the water for you," said Sack Todd. "We don't know as you deserve it, but we don't want to be mean."

As he spoke he and Gasper Pold held down a jug containing not more than two quarts.

"Not a very big supply," grumbled Tom. "We'll want a good deal more down here. This is a regular sweatbox."

"You don't have to stay any longer than you wish," answered the ex-counterfeiter, with a sickly grin.

"Ven do ve git somedings to eat?" asked Hans.

"In the morning."

This was all those above said, and soon the hatch was shut down and fastened and Todd and Pold walked slowly away.

"They didn't seem to care much whether we surrendered or not," remarked Sam.

"That makes me more suspicious than ever," answered Dick. "Boys, Dan Baxter may have been acting on the square after all."

"Catch Dan doing that!" retorted Tom. "Why, it isn't in him, Dick."

"I don't know about that. He is bad, I know, but he may not be as much of a villain as these men are. I am going to examine the contents of this jug."

All gathered around while Dick cleaned out the tumbler and then filled it with the liquid from the jug. The water looked fairly clear, although presently something like oil began to float on top. Dick put his tongue to this and found it sweetish-bitter.

"This has certainly been dosed," said the eldest Rover. "I wouldn't take a drink of it for a good deal."

"Then Baxter must have told the truth," said Sam. "I think I know how the matter stands. Baxter got scared at what the men wanted to do, and so started in to head them off. I believe I'll take a small drink of that other water."

He did so, and the others followed, nobody, however, drinking more than half a tumbler of the liquid. This served to quench the worst of their thirst.

"Later on, if the water doesn't affect us, we can drink more," said Tom. "If Dan Baxter really did mean well it's a great credit to him, no matter how bad he is otherwise."

All sat down and talked in low tones. The night was now well advanced, yet nobody felt like sleeping. Suddenly Dick leaped up, considerably excited.

"I've got it, fellows! Maybe we can outwit them at their own game," he cried.

"How?" asked the others.

"Perhaps that water was drugged and was given to us to put us to sleep. If we pretend to be overcome it may throw them off their guard, and that will give us another chance to gain possession of the vessel. What do you say if we lie down and pretend to be asleep when they open the hatch?"

"All right, I am willing," answered Tom. "There is no excitement in being cooped up in this hot place. Tell you what I'll do, to force matters. You lie down and begin to snore and I'll pull the whistle. Then, when they come, I'll demand to know what is wrong with you and pitch over myself. Then we can see what happens next."

So it was arranged, and half an hour later Sam, Dick, and Hans stretched out on the engineroom floor as if completely dead to the world. Then Tom gave the whistle half a dozen sharp tugs. This brought Todd, Pold, Jeffers, and Dan Baxter to the hatchway in a hurry.

"What's the row?" demanded Gasper Pold, looking down curiously.

"My brothers," came thickly from Tom, as he reeled around.

"What did you—you—do to them? My head—like—top! You—must—must—Oh!" And then Tom sank down on a bench, slipped to the floor, and lay beside Sam.

"He's poisoned!" shrieked Dan Baxter, and his face grew as white as a sheet.

"Shut up!" muttered Sack Todd. "The dose won't kill him."

"Reckon they are all laid out," was Gasper Pold's comment, as he peered down the hatchway. "I'll go down and make sure." And he passed down the iron ladder, pistol in hand.

"How about it?" came from the mate of the Dogstar.

"Stiff as corpses," was the brutal answer. "I tell you, that dope did the business."

"Are any of them dead?" asked Dan Baxter, hoarsely.

"I don't think so," was the careless answer. "No, they are all breathing," went on Pold.

Sack Todd came down, followed by the mate of the Dogstar, and all gazed coldly at the four youths lying on the hard floor around the machinery. Dan Baxter remained at the top of the ladder, shaking as if with the palsy.

"How long do you calculate they'll remain in this condition?" asked Todd, turning to Pold.

"Ten or twelve hours at least," was the answer. "And maybe they won't get over it for twenty-four."

"Any bad effects?"

"Well, sometimes that dope paralyzes a man's tongue for six months or a year."

"Phew! That's pretty rough."

"Once in a great while the paralysis doesn't go away at all."

"In that case, these boys will have it in for you,—if they ever get their hands on you," said Sid Jeffers, with a wicked leer.

The men talked among themselves for several minutes and then agreed to take the boys up on deck and place them in two of the staterooms off the cabin.

"They'll have to have more air than here," said Gasper Pold. "Otherwise they'll surely die on our hands."

Dan Baxter was called on to assist, and did so with his knees fairly shaking together. He thought that our friends had surely drank of the dosed water and were in a stupor next to death.

"And if they die, they'll say I was as guilty as the rest!" he groaned to himself. "Oh, I wish I was out of this!"

It was no easy matter to get the three Rovers and Hans on deck and to the staterooms. Here our friends were placed two on a berth, and, for the time being, left to themselves.

"Boys, we have had a narrow escape," whispered Dick, when he at last thought it safe to speak.

"That's the truth," came from Sam. "And we have Dan Baxter to thank for it!" he added. "I can't understand that part of it."

"I think I can," answered Tom. "Baxter is bad enough, but he didn't go in for poisoning us. I am glad to know he isn't quite so heartless as that."

"Dem fellers ought to be all hung, ain't it!" was Hans' comment.

"The question is, What are we to do next?" asked Tom.

"That question is not so easily answered," returned his elder brother. "I know what I should like to do."

"What, Dick?" asked Sam.

"I'd like to make all of the gang prisoners."

"Exactly!" exclaimed Tom, in a low voice. "But can it be done?"

"I don't know. For the present let us play 'possum and find out."

"Vot kind of a game vos dot possum?" asked Hans innocently. "I ton't dink we got dime to play some games," he added, seriously.

"Dick means to lay low," explained Sam.

"Vot, lay under der peds?"

"No, keep quiet and watch out."

"Oh! All right, I done me dot kvick enough," said Hans, and fell back on the berth and shut his eyes.

"You fellows keep quiet while I investigate," said the eldest Rover.

"It is so late some of the crowd may have gone to sleep. If so, we may have a chance to capture the others first."

So it was arranged, and making certain that his pistol was still in his pocket, Dick slid from the berth, tiptoed his way to the stateroom door, and, opening it slowly and cautiously, peered out.

One look into the cabin of the Mermaid told him the apartment was empty. There were two more staterooms, connected, as were those the boys were occupying. With a heart that beat rather violently, Dick stepped to the door of one of these staterooms. From within came a deep and regular snoring.

"Somebody is asleep in there," he mused. "Who can it be?"

With great care he peered into the room. On the berth rested one of the sailors from the Dogstar and on the floor rested the other, both evidently much the worse for liquor.

The door to the second stateroom was wide open and Dick caught sight of a form on the berth in there. It was Dan Baxter. The bully was not asleep but was tossing about, as if in either mental or physical distress. As Dick looked at him he suddenly started up, turned around, and stared.

"Dick Rover!" he screamed. "Are you alive, or is it a—a ghost?"

CHAPTER XXVI

TURNING THE TABLES

"Be quiet, Baxter," said Dick, softly but firmly. "Don't you dare to make another sound."

"I—I thought you were—were—asleep," faltered the former bully of Putnam Hall. "That you—"

"That he had drank the poisoned water, eh?"

"Ye—es."

"We did not. We took your advice and left it alone."

"Then when they brought you up out of the engine room—"

"We were shamming, that's all. But I haven't got time to explain everything, Baxter. Where are the others?"

"On deck, or down in the engine room, I guess—all but the two beasts in there," and Baxter pointed to the overcome sailors.

"What brought you in here? Were you going to sleep?"

"Sleep! I—I couldn't sleep, Dick; honestly I couldn't!"

"Why?"

"Because I—I—But what's the use, you won't believe me." And Dan Baxter hung his head for a moment.

"Maybe I will. Tell me why."

"I came away from them because I was sick of their doings, that's why. I—I am sick of all of it,—sick in body and in mind, too."

"You didn't want to see us doped, as they call it?"

"No! no!"

"And that is why you warned us and gave us that good water?"

"Yes."

"Dan, you're a little bit more of a real man than I thought you were. I thought you were willing to do anything against me and my brothers."

"Well, I was once, but now—But what's the use of talking, you won't believe me. And why should you? I've been against you ever since we first met."

"That's the straight truth, Dan, and you've done some pretty mean and desperate things."

"I don't know why I did them, Dick—honestly I don't. Lots of times I knew you and your brothers were right and I was wrong. But the Old Nick got in me and I—well, you know how I acted. Now I'm an outcast—nobody decent wants to have anything to do with me. Even my own father—" Dan Baxter stopped short.

"See here, Dan, I haven't time to talk now," said Dick, after a short and painful pause. "I didn't expect this of you. The whole question just now is this, Are you going to fight or keep quiet?"

"Are you going to fight those others?"

"Yes, if it becomes necessary."

"I don't want to fight any more."

"Then will you keep quiet?"

"I will. But, Dick—"

"Well?"

"If you capture those men, are you going to hand them over to the police?"

"Certainly."

"And hand me over, too?" And again Dan Baxter hung his head.

"Don't you deserve it?"

"I suppose so. And still I—er—I thought you might give me another chance. Oh, that's what I want, another chance! You know how my father has reformed. I want to reform, too. I want to go away somewhere and begin all over again."

"Dan, come with me."

"Where to?"

"To the others. You can talk with them while I take a look on deck."

The former bully of Putnam Hall demurred but Dick insisted, and soon the pair had joined Sam, Tom, and Hans.

"Talk to him," said Dick. "I'll be back soon," and then he left and made his way up the companionway to the deck of the steam yacht.

His heart was in a strange tumult. That Dan Baxter should want to reform was a surprise of which he had never dreamed. Could the former bully be playing a part?

"He's sly enough," he reasoned. "And yet his eyes had a look in them that I never saw before. He looked like a worried wild animal, that doesn't know how to turn or what to do. He's down here all alone among strangers, and evidently he has found out that Sack Todd and the rest aren't his sort. Well, if he wants to reform I shan't put anything in his way. But I am not going to give him too much rope—just yet."

Having gained the deck of the vessel, Dick looked around cautiously. It was a dark night, the stars being hidden by clouds. He crept along slowly.

"Well, you'll have to give me a pointer or two about the engine," Dick heard Sack Todd exclaim. "I thought I knew how to run it, but I reckon I was mistaken."

"Oh, why not let that go just now," growled the mate of the Dogstar in return. "We've got to make sure of those boys first, and get some sleep, too."

"It won't take but a few minutes to explain about the engine," said Gasper Pold. "I ran one once for six weeks."

"Seems to me you have dabbled in a little bit of everything," observed Sack Todd.

"So I have."

The three men were near the pilot house, but came away and started for the hatchway leading down into the engine room. They had to pass close to where Dick was crouching and the eldest Rover hardly dared to breathe, so fearful was he of discovery.

Presently Dick saw the three men go down the iron ladder, one after another. As they did this, a sudden idea came into his head.

"I'll do it!" he told himself, and sneaked forward with the silence and quickness of a cat.

The hatch still lay beside the opening, with the hooks that had been used to fasten it down. It was heavy and Dick wondered if he could move and fasten it quick enough.

"I wish Sam or Tom was here to help me," he thought.

As he started to raise the hatch a sudden puff of wind made the mast creak loudly. This alarmed the men below and Sack Todd started up the ladder.

"We ought to have somebody on guard," he said, so loudly that Dick heard him. "I don't trust that Baxter very much."

"All right," answered Gasper Pold. "You go to the cabin, and—"

He broke off short as a cry came from Sack Todd. The ex-counterfeiter had caught sight of Dick as the latter was raising the hatch to drop it in place.

"Hi!" yelled Sack Todd, and then let out a scream as the hatch hit him on the head.

"Down you go!" answered Dick and leaped on top of the hatch to force it into place. One of Sack Todd's fingers was caught and pinched and he let out another yell. But he kept his footing on the iron ladder and thus held the hatch up several inches.

"What's up?" came from Sid Jeffers.

"They are trying to shut the hatch! Help me!"

"What!" roared Gasper Pold, and sprang up beside the ex-counterfeiter.

"Tom! Sam! Hans!" yelled Dick, at the top of his lungs. "Help! Quick!"

He continued to call out and at the same time did all in his power to force the hatch into place. He was sprawled on top, and no sooner did he get one end down than the other bobbed up. Then he heard Gasper Pold cry out:

"Look out! I am going to fire!"

"Don't hit me," cautioned Sack Todd.

"If you fire, so will I," answered Dick, "and you'll get the worst of it."

"Hang the luck! We didn't disarm them!" muttered Pold.

By this time Tom was coming up on deck, followed by Sam. Hans was told to remain behind, to keep his eyes on Dan Baxter.

As soon as Sam and Tom saw the situation they leaped to Dick's assistance. Tom saw Sack Todd's shoulder under the hatch and gave it a vigorous kick. This caused the man to lose his balance on the iron ladder and he went down a step. At the same time Gasper Pold fired.

"Oh, I am hit!" groaned the ex-counterfeiter, and fell in a heap on the head of Sid Jeffers. Then the hatch came into place with a thud and in a twinkling the three Rovers secured it.

"We have them! We have them!" cried Sam, in delight. "Good for you, Dick! That was a clever move."

"Run down and make certain that other door is fast," said Dick, and away went Sam with Tom at his heels. They came back in less than two minutes.

"It's fast," said Tom. "We've got them in as tight a box as they had us."

CHAPTER XXVII

DAN BAXTER'S REPENTANCE

The three Rover boys could scarcely believe their senses. Here they were once more in full possession of the Mermaid so far as the deck and cabin were concerned—and those who had sought to make them prisoners were prisoners themselves.

"This is where the biter got bit," remarked Tom. "Say, I feel so good I could almost dance."

"Sack Todd got shot," said Dick. "I'd like to know if it is serious."

"Well, I am not very sorry for him," said Sam. "He's a thoroughly bad egg."

"We want to make certain of Dan Baxter," went on the eldest Rover. "He may fool Hans."

They walked toward the cabin and ran down the companionway. At the lower doorway they paused and then Tom grinned.

On one side of the room was Dan Baxter with his hands in the air. On the other side was Hans, with a pistol in each hand.

"Ton't dare to mofe," Hans was saying. "Of you do I vos put ox-actly fourteen shots into your poty, ain't it!"

"I am not moving," grumbled Baxter. "Didn't I tell you I am sick of the whole thing, Dutchy? I don't want to fight, or anything."

"Tan Paxter, you chust remember dot old saying, beoples vot lif in glass houses ton't got no right to tell fish stories," answered Hans, gravely.

"Hans, that's a good one!" roared Tom, coming forward. "Say, you're a whole regiment in yourself, ain't you?"

"Yah, I vos so goot like ten or sefenteen soljers, alretty!" answered the German youth, proudly. "Paxter, he ton't got avay from me, not much!"

Hans lowered his pistols and Dan Baxter was glad enough to put down his hands. Dick glanced into the staterooms and saw that the two sailors were still sleeping heavily.

"We'll throw them down into the hold," said the eldest Rover. "That will keep them out of mischief, when they awake."

"Vot apout dem men?" asked Hans, anxiously.

"All prisoners," answered Sam.

"Prisoners!" ejaculated Dan Baxter.

"Yes, Dan, they are prisoners, down in the engine room," answered Dick. "We've given them the same dose they gave us."

"Then you are in possession once more?"

"Yes—as far as it goes. And I want to talk to you as soon as we've disposed of these sailors," added Dick.

"Shall I help you carry them out?"

"Do you want to?"

"If you wish it."

"Mind you, I don't want any trick played, Dan."

"I won't play any trick, Dick—I give you my word."

"This is a serious situation and we don't propose to take any more chances. We are on top and we mean to stay on top," added the eldest Rover.

While Hans held a lantern, the three Rovers and Dan Baxter carried the two sailors through the cabin and out on the deck. Tom was working with the former bully of Putnam Hall and declared afterward that he never felt so queer in his life. But Baxter worked with a will and did his full share of lifting.

The hatch to the hold was not far off and the men were put down without great trouble. Then the hatch was closed and fastened.

"Now, Dan, you are the only enemy we have who is at liberty," said Dick, turning to the big youth. "I want to know exactly what you propose to do."

"What I do will depend a good deal on what you do," was the somewhat low answer. "I know I am in your power. But I'd like you to remember one thing—about how I warned you not to drink the drugged water and how I brought you some good water."

"I am not going to forget that."

"That's a point to your credit, Dan," said Sam.

"If it hadn't been for that I—er—I don't know where you'd be now. As I said before, I've been pretty bad—but not quite as bad as that."

"Do you think we ought to let you go for what you did for us?" asked Tom, who never wanted to beat about the bush.

"I don't know as you ought to do that—but I'd like you to do it. I'd like to have the chance to go away—far away—and strike out fresh. My father wants me to do it—he's written me three letters about it. He wants me to go to the Hawaiian Islands, or the Philippines, or to Australia. He says—but I don't suppose you are interested in what he writes."

"I am," answered Dick, promptly.

"He spoke of what you did for him and he says I—well, I ought to be ashamed to keep up the old enmity after what happened—after you saved his life. I—er—I guess he's right—and I am sick of it all."

"Well, I hope you stay sick of it—I mean sick of doing wrong," said Sam.

"Maybe I will—I don't know and I am not going to promise. But I am sick enough of being here, among such rough men as Sack Todd and Gasper Pold and that crowd of counterfeiters that was captured. I haven't had any real comfort for months."

"I don't believe a criminal ever feels real comfortable," said Tom. "How can he, when he knows the officers of the law are constantly after him?"

"There is something in that. When I go to bed I generally dream of being caught and dragged to prison. And those men always wanted me to drink, and I don't care much for liquor."

"Then cut it out—cut it out by all means," said Dick. "You can't do better."

"And there is another thing," went on Dan Baxter. "I don't feel well—everything I eat lately goes against me, and sometimes I'm in a regular fever. I ought to rest somewhere, I suppose, and have a good doctor attend me. But I can't do anything to make me feel better chasing around like this."

After that Dan Baxter told a good deal more about himself—how he had been knocking around in all sorts of questionable places and how the dissipation had grown very distasteful to him. It had certainly ruined his health, and his eyes had a hollow, feverish look in them that made his appearance rather pitiable.

"You are certainly run down," said Dick, "and unless you take extra good care of yourself you'll be flat on your back with some serious illness. But the question still is, Dan, What are we to do with you?"

"I know what I'd like you to do."

"What?"

"Let me land somewhere where I am not known, so that the officers of the law can't get hold of me. Do that, and I'll promise to go far away and never trouble you again."

"I don't think that would be right," said Tom. "We might be willing, but we can't assist a criminal to escape—that's a crime in itself."

"Then you won't let me go?"

"Tom is right, we can't do it, legally. Personally I'd be willing to let you go," said Dick.

"So would I—if you really wanted to do better," came from Sam.

"Yah, I ton't stand in nopody's vay," added Hans. "I vos glad to see a man make a goot poy of himselluf!"

There was an awkward pause. Twice Dan Baxter started to speak and checked himself. They almost looked for one of his former wild outbreaks, but it did not come. He hung his head low.

"All right—have your way," he whispered, hoarsely, and dropped into a chair. "I am done fighting. I'll take my medicine, no matter how bitter it is."

"Perhaps we can make matters a little easy for you," said Dick, in a gentle tone. "I am sure none of us want to see you suffer—if you want to reform."

"Of course we'll be easy," said Sam, and Tom and Hans nodded.

"Well, if you'll do—What's that?"

Dan Baxter broke off short and all in the cabin listened. There was a thud and a crash, followed by another crash.

"They are trying to break out of the engine room!" yelled Dick. "Come, we must stop them!" And he started for the deck, and all of the crowd went after him.

CHAPTER XXVIII

HATCHWAY AND DOOR

The news that the men were trying to break out of the engine room was true. Gasper Pold and Sid Jeffers had gotten a long piece of iron pipe and with this they were hammering at the hatch. One of the fastenings was already off and the others much weakened.

"Stop!" cried Dick, rushing up. "Stop, or we'll open fire on you!"

"We are bound to get out and you can't stop us!" yelled back Gasper Pold, and started to mount the iron ladder with a long wrench. This instrument he placed under a corner of the hatch and began to pry the wooden barrier upward.

"Not so fast!" sang out Tom, and rushing up he sprawled over the hatch and caught the end of the wrench. "One good wrench deserves another!" he muttered, his love of fun coming to the surface even in such a pitch of excitement, and with that he gave the wrench a wrench that brought it from Pold's grip and allowed the hatch to fall into place.

"All aboard!" sang out Tom, and Dick, Sam, and Hans leaped on top of the hatch. "Nothing like holding 'em down!"

"Let us up!" roared Sid Jeffers, and a moment later a pistol shot rang out and a bullet came crashing through the hatch, but its force was so spent it merely bounced against Han's trouser leg.

"I vos hit! I vos hit!" shrieked the German youth, dancing around. "I vos a teat boy alretty!"

"Hans, are you really hit?" asked Dick, in alarm.

"Yah, but—I guess it ton't vos much," added Hans sheepishly, as he realized that no damage had been done.

"Here, hold it down with this," cried Dan Baxter and came forward with two capstan bars. These were placed across the hatch and the four boys took their stations at the ends of the bars. Thus they managed to get out of firing range of those below.

"This is certainly growing interesting," was Dick's comment, as there was a moment's suspension of hostilities. "I hardly know what to do next."

"If you don't let us up we'll blow up the ship!" yelled Gasper Pold. He was in a terrible fury.

"If you blow up the ship, you'll go up with her," answered Sam.

"Gracious, vill da do dot?" asked Hans, in alarm.

"No, they'll not be so foolish," answered Tom. "They value their worthless hides too much."

"You've nearly killed Sack Todd and we'll have you arrested for it," went on Gasper Pold.

"You'll be nearly killed if you don't look out," answered Dick. "We are in possession and we mean to keep in possession."

"You can't run the boat without the engine."

"Yes, we can, for the sails are ready for use. We won't have to run, though. By morning we expect to sight some other vessel and then we'll get help."

"What have you done with those two sailors?" asked Sid Jeffers.

"Put them where they can't do any harm."

"Where is Baxter?" asked Pold.

"That is for you to find out."

"I am here," said the former bully of Putnam Hall.

"Helping that crowd?"

"Yes. I don't want anything more to do with you, or with Sack Todd either."

"The young skunk!" muttered the mate of the Dogstar. "I told you I didn't like his looks."

"Say, Dick Rover, let us talk this matter over," said Gasper Pold, calming down a little. "If you'll be reasonable I am sure we can come to terms that will be satisfactory all around."

"I don't think so."

"This craft is worth a lot of money, so the mate of the Dogstar says, and there is no reason why all of us shouldn't make a neat pile out of her."

"Do you want us to go in partnership with you?" asked Tom, in disgust.

"That's it, and if you will, we'll say nothing about your hurting Sack Todd."

"Is he bad?" asked Sam.

"He is bad enough. We want to get out so that he can have proper attention and medicine."

"Better give him some of that doctored water," suggested Tom, grimly.

"Don't get fresh, young man!"

"I think you are the one who is fresh!" retorted Tom. "Do you think we are going to train with such fellows as you? Not much!"

"Then you won't make terms?"

"No," came from the three Rovers.

At this the men at the foot of the iron ladder muttered something that our friends could not catch. The rascals were furious and wanted to do some more shooting, but did not dare, fearing shots in return.

"Will you let Sack Todd have some water?" asked Pold, presently.

"There is good water in the bucket," answered Dick.

"That's gone."

"Then you'll have to wait until later for more."

"Todd has got to have water."

At this announcement the boys looked questioningly at each other.

"It may be true," said Dick. "I shouldn't want the man to die just because we had refused him water."

"It may be a trick, just to get the hatch open again," put in Dan Baxter. "If I were you I wouldn't trust them. I know that crowd better than you do."

"You can have water in the morning," called down Dick. "In the meantime you keep quiet and do what you can for Todd. If you don't keep quiet you'll get the worst of it."

"Wait till I get my hands on you!" came in the hoarse voice of Sack Todd. "I'll pulverize you!"

"He's a long way from being dead, by his voice," said Dick. "I reckon he was playing off on us." And this was largely true. Sack Todd's wound was painful but by no means serious.

It must be confessed that the boys hardly knew how to proceed. But presently Dick remembered where he had seen some hooks and nails and he sent Dan Baxter for these. When they were brought he calmly proceeded to fasten the extra hooks to the hatch and then hook them fast to the deck.

"What are you doing now?" yelled Gasper Pold, and when he was told he muttered things I do not care to mention on these pages.

"Now, Sam and Tom, you remain on guard here, while the rest of us go and secure that door below," said Dick.

"It is secure," said Tom.

"Yes, I know, but some extra cross bars won't do any harm."

"Want me to help?" asked Baxter.

"You can come along," said Dick, not altogether willing to leave the former bully out of sight.

He hurried to the door in question, one leading from the back of the engine room into something of a storeroom. The door was fastened by two ordinary bolts.

"I'll soon fix that!" said the eldest Rover. "Dan, you hold the lantern. Hans, bring that piece of board here."

The board was brought, and Dick began to nail it fast, directly over the door. He had still another nail to drive when there came an unexpected crash on the other side.

"All together!" yelled the voice of Gasper Pold. "Now then, with a will!"

Another mighty crash followed and then a third. With this the door flew from its hinges, and over it came, hurling Hans flat on his back. Then Dick found himself confronted by Pold, Jeffers, and Sack Todd, each with a weapon ready for use.

CHAPTER XXIX

AN EXCITING TIME ALL AROUND

"We've got him! Down with him!" roared Sack Todd, as he leaped over the fallen door and made a grab for Dick.

For the instant Dick did not know what to do, then he stepped backward and at the same time attempted to draw his pistol.

"No, you don't!" yelled Gasper Pold, and aimed a blow at Dick's head with an iron bar he carried.

Had the blow landed as intended, the eldest Rover might have had his skull crushed in. But as the iron bar was descending Dan Baxter made a quick jump to Pold's side, gave him a shove and hurled him flat.

"Stop it!" cried the former bully of Putnam Hall. "Do you hear? Do you want to kill somebody?"

"So you're against us, eh?" yelled Sack Todd. "Well, we'll fix you!"

He tore a pistol from his pocket and started to aim it at Baxter. But the latter was now on the alert and, whirling around, he caught Sack Todd by the coat collar with one hand and with the other raised the pistol up into the air. It went off, but the bullet merely plowed its way into the woodwork of the ship.

By this time Hans had managed to scramble from beneath the fallen door. The German youth had not been hurt very much but his "Dutch blood" was up, and throwing prudence to the wind he sailed in vigorously, hitting Pold a blow in the stomach with his fist, and kicking the mate of the Dogstar in the shin with his heavy shoe. Then he caught hold of Pold's iron bar and began to wrestle for its possession.

"You dink I vos noddings put a poy, hey!" he snorted. "I show you, ain't it! You pig loafer!" And he ran Pold up against a partition and

DAN BAXTER MADE A QUICK JUMP TO POLD'S SIDE, GAVE HIM
A SHOVE AND HURLED HIM FLAT.

got the iron bar directly under the rascal's throat so that the fellow was in danger of strangling.

Sid Jeffers had now turned his attention to Dick, and blows were given and taken freely between the pair. The noise made was considerable, and this finally reached the ears of Sam and Tom.

"Something is wrong!" cried Tom. "I'll go and see. If you want me back whistle as loudly as you can." And he was off like a shot.

The sight that met Tom's gaze at first almost stupefied him. He came upon Sack Todd and Dan Baxter fighting hand to hand in a passageway leading to the deck. Sack Todd had fired one shot which had grazed Dan's left cheek. But now the youth had the man against the wall and was banging his head against it again and again.

"You will shoot me, eh?" cried Baxter. "You're a villain if ever there was one, Sack Todd. I am bad enough but I'm not as dirty and black as you. Take that, and that, and that!"

"Hi! let up! You'll smash my head!" roared the ex-counterfeiter, but Dan Baxter paid no attention until one blow caused Sack Todd to lose consciousness and sink down in a heap.

Tom had already passed on and was in time to aid Dick. Coming up to the side of Sid Jeffers he hit the mate of the Dogstar a stinging blow in the ear and then another in the chin. Dick at the same time struck the rascal in the eye, and Jeffers staggered back, tripped over the fallen door, and landed heavily on the floor. At once Tom sat down on him, pulling out his pistol as he did so.

"Now keep quiet or something worse will happen," he said, and the mate of the Dogstarunderstood and subsided.

With the fall of Sack Todd, Dan Baxter turned back to aid the others. He saw Sid Jeffers go down and then ran toward Hans.

"You might as well give up," he said to Gasper Pold. "They've got the best of your crowd."

"Yes, and you helped them," said Pold, sullenly. "Just wait. I'll fix you for this!"

The noise continuing, Sam had left his post and arrived on the scene. He ran off for a rope and with this Sack Todd was bound

hands and feet. Seeing this, Gasper Pold and the mate of the Dogstar retreated again into the engine room.

"Put up that door!" cried Dick, and without delay it was raised and put in place and then fastened in such a manner that it was next to impossible to budge it. Then they ran on deck and fastened down the hatch. After that they gave Todd their attention.

When he came to his senses the ex-counterfeiter raved wildly and demanded that he be set free. He was particularly bitter against Dan Baxter.

"I'll fix you," he said. "Wait till we get into court. I'll have a fine story to tell about you." To this Baxter did not reply although he turned very pale.

Seeing they could do little with Sack Todd, the Rovers decided to put him down in the hold with the sailors and this was done. Then the party with Baxter gathered on deck to discuss the situation.

"Talk about a strenuous night," exclaimed Tom. "I don't think it could be more strenuous than it has been."

"Dan, I want to say right now that you have helped us a great deal," said Dick, turning to the big youth. "But for you we might have lost that battle."

"Dot is so," said Hans. "You vos tone splendidly alretty!"

With two of the enemy in possession of the engine room, it was of course impossible to run the machinery of the steam yacht, and this being so our friends decided to wait until daylight before attempting to make another move.

"It is after three o'clock," said Dick. "We may as well get what rest we can. We can take turns at remaining on guard," and so it was decided. But it must be said that nobody got much sleep, so great was the general excitement.

While he was on guard Dick had a long private talk with Dan Baxter, and for once the former bully of Putnam Hall opened his heart completely. He had been knocking around "from pillar to post" so long that he was utterly discouraged and scarcely cared what happened. Since his father had reformed, and he had lost the compan-

ionship of Lew Flapp, he had been traveling among strangers and not a one of them had proved worth knowing, as he expressed it.

"I was a great big fool that I didn't turn over a new leaf when my father did," he said. "I had a chance then to do something for myself. Now I am so deep in the mud I don't know how I'll ever get out."

"I am certainly sorry for you, Dan—especially after what you did for our crowd to-night. If you really want to turn over a new leaf I am willing to help you all I can. But you know how the law stands— we can't let you go after what has happened in the past. If you come up for trial, though, I'll be as easy as I can on you, and I know the others will be easy, too. Perhaps, as you are young, you'll get off with a light sentence, and then you'll have a chance to reform after that."

At this Dan Baxter hung his head.

"It's a terrible disgrace—to go to prison," he answered, in a low tone. "But my father had to go through it, and I guess I am worse than he is." He heaved a deep sigh. "Well, I'll try to stand it."

"If it gets as far as that, when you come out, Dan, you come straight to me and I'll help you."

"Will you do that, Dick?" asked the former bully, eagerly, and for the instant his face brightened.

"I will, and there is my hand on it," and then the two who had been enemies for so many years shook hands. After that Dan Baxter continued to talk about himself. He seemed anxious to unburden his heart, and Dick allowed him to proceed and listened with interest to the recital.

As soon as it was daylight the Rovers, Hans, and Baxter went on deck to decide upon the all-important question of what to do next. Dick had inspected the sails and found them in trim for use, and presently they set sail and once more the steam yacht was headed for Tampa Bay. There was a stiff breeze blowing, and although the craft made no such speed as when under steam she went along right well, and they were all content.

About the middle of the forenoon they heard a thumping on the hatch over the engine room. Pold and Jeffers wanted something to

eat and to drink, and wanted to make terms, but they told the rascals they would have to wait until land or some vessel was sighted. They also got a call from Sack Todd and the sailors who had revived from their stupor, but decided to let these fellows wait also.

"The sailors have done us no harm," said Dick. "But a waiting spell will do them good, after such a beastly spree."

It was one o'clock, and Hans was preparing dinner for all on deck when Tom gave a cry.

"A small steamer is approaching!" he said. "Hadn't we better signal her?"

"By all means," answered Dick. "Let us steer directly for her, too." And this was done.

The vessel approaching proved to be nothing more than a regular gulf tug, carrying eight people. As it came closer Sam, who had a spy-glass, gave a shout:

"What do you think! There are Fred and Songbird, and yes, there is Harold Bird, too! Oh, how glad I am that they are safe!"

CHAPTER XXX

HOMEWARD BOUND—CONCLUSION

The report was true, the tug contained Fred, Songbird, and Harold Bird, and as soon as these three made out who were on board of the Mermaid they set up a cheer. Then the sails on the steam yacht were lowered and the tug came alongside. In a minute more Fred was scrambling on deck, followed by the others.

"Alive! All of you!" cried Fred. "Oh, this is the best news yet!"

"And we are glad to see you alive too," cried Tom. "We were afraid the Mascotte had been lost."

"Well, we came close to it," said Songbird. "And when we got in to port some of the passengers had the captain arrested for ill treatment. But we didn't wait for that. We were wild to know what had become of you, and so we chartered this tug and began a hunt. You were lucky to be picked up by such a nice craft as this."

"We weren't picked up,—we picked ourselves up," answered Dick.

"Why, what do you mean?" asked Harold Bird, in puzzled tones.

"We found this steam yacht on the water deserted—not a soul on board."

"You don't mean it!" ejaculated Fred. "What's her name?"

"The Mermaid."

"Creation!" shouted Harold Bird. "Why, that's the steam yacht was advertised in all the newspapers some weeks ago. She was missing, and the club that owns her offered a reward of five thousand dollars for information leading to her return."

"Well, we picked her up as a derelict," said Tom. "And we'll claim salvage accordingly. But how did she disappear?"

"It's a long story. She was left in charge of an old man, and he went

off and got intoxicated. Then a storm came up and they found the old man in a rowboat and the steam yacht missing. She must have blown and drifted far away on the gulf. But it's queer she wasn't sighted before."

"Maybe she was, but nobody thought she was deserted," said Sam, and his idea was probably true.

Thus far Dan Baxter had kept in the background. When he came forward there was more astonishment, and our friends had to tell about the arrival of Sack Todd and the others, and of what had been done since.

"I want you to understand that Dan helped us a great deal," said Dick, to Fred and Songbird. "He isn't the fellow he was. He has changed so you would hardly know he was the same person. I think he is really on the right track at last."

"It seems too wonderful to be true," was Fred's comment.

Dan Baxter was much interested in meeting Harold Bird, and while the others were talking in one part of the deck he called the young Southerner to one side.

"Mr. Bird, you know who I am, and I suppose you have no use for me," began the former bully. "I am sorry I went in with those men who stole your gasoline launch. If I had my choice again I shouldn't do such a thing. I am very sorry, and I am glad you got your boat back. But I want to speak to you about something else. I was going to write you a letter when I got the chance, but I'd rather tell you what I know."

"What you know?" repeated Harold Bird, somewhat puzzled.

"Yes. Since I have been traveling with Gasper Pold and Sack Todd I have learned a great deal, and much of it concerns yourself and your father."

"My father!" gasped the young Southerner.

"Yes."

"What do you know of him? Is he alive?"

"I think he is—at least Gasper Pold said he was."

"Pold! What does he know about it? Where is my father?"

"As near as I know, your father is in Mexico, at a place called Trox-apocca. He is somewhat out of his mind, and Pold told Sack Todd he was working around a hotel there, doing all sorts of odd jobs. He goes by the name of Bangs—why, I don't know."

"Is it possible! I must look into this without delay."

"And then there is something else I want to tell you. I heard Todd and Pold talking about it when they thought they were alone. Todd accused Pold of having killed an old man, a hunter, in the woods, because the old hunter had vowed to expose one of Pold's lottery swindles. It came out in the talk that Pold had really done the deed and had put the dead hunter on a rock, where he was shot at by your father. Your father didn't hit the body, but he thought he did, and thinking he had killed this old man was what made your father crazy."

"I know it! I know it!" cried Harold Bird. "What a vile deed to do! And did Pold admit his guilt?"

"He did, but he warned Sack Todd to keep quiet about it. That was one of the things that turned me against that gang. They were altogether too bad for me. From that moment on I was sorry I had gone in with them."

"This fairly staggers me, Baxter. You—you must help me prove this—after I have found my father, or before."

"I will, Mr. Bird—I'll do all I can to make things right again," answered Dan Baxter, earnestly.

When the others heard of Dan Baxter's revelation they were almost as much astonished as Harold Bird. They were glad to learn that there was now a likelihood of clearing the young Southerner's father of the crime of which he had been accused, and all trusted he would soon be able to locate Mr. Bird and nurse him back to mental and physical health.

Those on the tug were called on board and then Sack Todd was allowed to come on deck, followed by the two sailors. All were made prisoners. Then Gasper Pold and Sid Jeffers came up and were handcuffed.

Gasper Pold was amazed to find himself confronted by Harold Bird, and when accused of the shooting of the old hunter broke down utterly. He thought Sack Todd had exposed him, and a bitter war of words between the pair followed.

"You have done me a splendid service, Baxter," said the young Southerner, after the excitement was over. "I shall not forget you. When the proper time comes, if you need legal aid, I'll see to it that you have a first-class lawyer."

"Thank you," answered the former bully, humbly. "I only did my duty, which I should have done long ago."

It was found that the Mermaid belonged to persons living at Mobile, and accordingly the steam yacht and the tug were headed for that port. The run did not take more than twenty-four hours and when the Mermaid appeared she created considerable excitement. One of the owners, James Morrison, soon came to take charge, in the name of the yacht club, and he assured Dick and the others that the club would pay anything that was fair for the return of the vessel.

"We have found one thing that bothered us," said Dick. "Perhaps you can explain it. In a locker we found a picture of Harold Bird and also a picture of his father."

"I know nothing of them. I did not know Mr. Bird at all."

"I will have Harold show you his father's photograph. Perhaps you'll recognize him."

The picture was shown and James Morrison uttered a cry of astonishment.

"I know that man, but his name was not Bird. It was Bangs. He worked on the yacht for awhile—queer sort of stick—and he left rather suddenly."

"It was Mr. Bird. He went crazy over some personal trouble, and Harold has been looking all over for him. He was last heard of in Mexico. But this clears up the mystery of the photographs," Dick added.

And now let me add a few words more and then bring to a close this tale of "The Rover Boys in Southern Waters."

As soon as they arrived at Mobile the Rover boys sent telegrams to their folks at home and also to the ladies and girls at the Bird plantation, telling of the safety of the entire party.

Sack Todd, Gasper Pold, Sid Jeffers, and the two sailors were locked up. Nobody attempted to have Dan Baxter arrested, nor did the former bully of Putnam Hall try to run away.

"I have made up my mind to take my medicine and I am going to do it," he said, almost stubbornly.

"What a change in him!" was Tom's comment. "The fellows at Putnam Hall won't believe it when we tell them."

"Here is the whole thing in a nutshell," said Sam. "Dan has found out that there is absolutely no happiness or satisfaction in being dishonest. Even when he had money he didn't enjoy it—he told me so himself. He said there was many a day when he would have preferred being with the old crowd, even without a cent in his pocket."

As soon as he could Harold Bird set off for Mexico. A week later he sent Dick Rover a telegram stating that he had found his father and was taking him home. It may be added here that, cleared of the suspicion that had hung over his name, Mr. Bird speedily recovered from his insanity, and became the prosperous planter he had been in years gone by.

When Sack Todd, Gasper Pold, and Sid Jeffers were brought to trial Dan Baxter was a witness against each one. For the shooting of the old hunter Pold received a life sentence in prison, and for their various misdeeds Todd and the mate of the Dogstar received ten and twenty years respectively. Solly Jackson was also a witness against Todd and Pold and was not prosecuted.

"What are you going to do about Dan Baxter?" asked Songbird of Dick, one day.

"I am going to do nothing," answered Dick, firmly. "If you want to prosecute him you can do so."

"He expects to be placed on trial."

"Well, he'll have to find somebody else to prosecute him."

"I shan't do anything, Dick. Why, he isn't the same chap he used to be. He's as meek as any fellow I ever met."

In the end nobody prosecuted Dan Baxter, and he was allowed to go his own way. The Rovers talked the matter over and one day they sent for the former bully and asked him how much money he had on hand.

"I've got exactly two dollars and a quarter," was the answer. "I am looking for work, but I haven't found anything yet," and Baxter's face grew red and he hung his head.

"We have made up a purse for you, Dan," said Dick, kindly. "Those folks who owned the yacht gave us ten thousand dollars for bringing her in safely. I have had a talk with our crowd, and we are going to stake you for a fresh start."

So speaking, Dick handed out a new pocketbook. But Dan Baxter put his hands behind him.

"Thank you very, very much," he said, huskily, "but I don't want you to—to give me a cent—not a cent, understand? If you want to make me a loan, well and good. But I shan't take it if it's a gift."

"Well, we'll call it a loan then," said Tom, who stood by.

"And you can pay up whenever you please," added Sam.

Dan Baxter took the pocketbook and opened it.

"Why, ifs full of bills!" he gasped.

"Yes, a thousand dollars, Dan. We want you to make a good start while you are at it," explained Dick.

The face of the former bully became a study. His eyes grew moist and his lips quivered. He had to turn away for a moment, for he could not control himself.

"You're the best fellows in the world—the very best," he murmured, presently. "A thousand dollars! And you were going to give it to me—not loan it to me! I'll never forget that, never, if I live to be a hundred. But I am not going to take all that money—it's too much of a temptation. Let me have a hundred as a loan, and that's all."

This he stuck to, and in the end the hundred dollars was counted out and Baxter placed it in his pocket.

"This will take me to Philadelphia," he said. "There I can get hold of some money that is rightfully mine, and then I'll return the loan. After that—well, after that I am going far away, to try to make a man of myself."

"We wish you luck, Dan," answered Dick, gravely.

"Indeed we do," added Sam and Tom.

There was an awkward silence. Then Dan Baxter pulled himself up, hesitated, and held out his hand.

"I don't know when we'll meet again," he said. "Good-by."

"Good-by," said each of the others and shook hands warmly.

The former bully walked to the doorway and there hesitated again.

"Please do me one favor," he said, his face growing red. "When you meet the Stanhopes and the Lanings tell them I am very sorry for what I did, and that I wouldn't do it again for the whole world. And tell Captain Putnam that, too." And then he went out, closing the door softly behind him. They listened to his footsteps, and as they died away each heaved a deep sigh.

"I am sorry for him," said Dick.

"I pity him from the bottom of my heart," came from Sam.

"And so do I," added Tom. "Poor chap, I hope he does make a man of himself." It was a long time before they saw Dan Baxter again.

What to do with the houseboat they did not know, but soon came a message from their Uncle Randolph, stating they might sell the craft. They found a ready purchaser at a fair price, and then joined the Stanhopes and the Lanings at the Bird plantation.

"Oh, how glad I am that you are safe!" cried Dora to Dick, when they met. "It seems an age since you went away."

"So it does—with so much happening," answered the eldest of the Rover boys.

"Are we going home now?" asked Sam.

"We'll have to," answered Tom. "We ought to be at our studies this minute."

"Yes, because you love study so!" cried Nellie, mischievously.

Two days later found them on a river steamer that was to take them up the Mississippi as far as St. Louis, where they were to take the Limited Express for New York.

"Well, I suppose our good times and our adventures are over now," said Sam. But he was mistaken. Good times and strange adventures still awaited them, and what some of these were will be told in the next volume of this series, to be entitled "The Rover Boys on the Farm; or, Last Days at Putnam Hall."

The whole party remained in St. Louis one day. Then they sped eastward on the Limited, and the following evening found them on their way to Valley Brook farm, the Stanhopes and Lanings having decided to stop off there for at least a day or two.

"It will feel fine to get home again," said Sam, as the train rolled into the Oak Run station. "Hurrah! here we are at last!"

"And there are father, Aunt Martha, and Uncle Randolph to meet us!" exclaimed Tom.

"Hullo, everybody!" called out Dick, and tumbled out of the train, to kiss his aunt and shake hands all around. "Home again, and glad of it!"

"And we are glad to see you all!" answered his father. And then there was general rejoicing, and here we will take our leave.

THE END

Printed in Great Britain
by Amazon

50891100R00098